BUNGALOW BY THE BAY

KAY CORRELL

ROSE QUARTZ PRESS

Published by Rose Quartz Press

080918

ISBN 978-1-944761-18-9

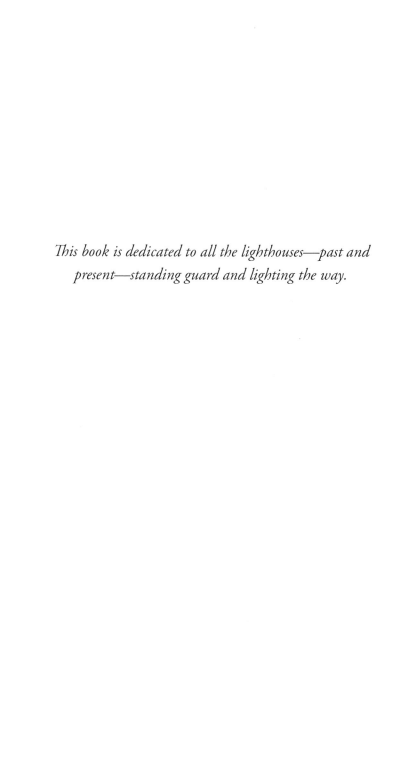

This book is dedicated to all the lighthouses—past and present—standing guard and lighting the way.

KAY'S BOOKS

Find more information on all my books at
kaycorrell.com

COMFORT CROSSING ~ THE SERIES
The Shop on Main - Book One
The Memory Box - Book Two
The Christmas Cottage - A Holiday Novella
(Book 2.5)
The Letter - Book Three
The Christmas Scarf - A Holiday Novella
(Book 3.5)
The Magnolia Cafe - Book Four
The Unexpected Wedding - Book Five

The Wedding in the Grove - (a crossover short story

between series - with Josephine and Paul from The Letter.)

LIGHTHOUSE POINT ~ THE SERIES
Wish Upon a Shell - Book One
Wedding on the Beach - Book Two
Love at the Lighthouse - Book Three
Cottage near the Point - Book Four
Return to the Island - Book Five
Bungalow by the Bay - Book Six

INDIGO BAY ~ A multi-author sweet romance series
Sweet Sunrise - Book Three
Sweet Holiday Memories - A short holiday story
Sweet Starlight - Book Nine

Sign up for my newsletter at my website *kaycorrell.com* to make sure you don't miss any new releases or sales.

CHAPTER 1

Courtney Davis slowly closed the door to the storage building by Magic Cafe. Her son, Bobby, had named it Happy House, and they *had* been very happy living there. A wave of sadness swept over her.

She locked the door, patted it affectionately, and slipped the key in her pocket. She was going to miss this place. It had been the first place she and Bobby had ever called home. Their little apartment in the front of the building had suited her just fine, but Tally and Eddie had insisted she and Bobby find a more suitable place to live.

Tally walked up and grabbed a bag sitting outside the door. "Let me help."

"You don't need to do that. I'll get it. I only have these last few loads."

"I want to help." Tally gathered up a laundry basket filled with odds and ends, plopped the bag into the basket, and perched the basket on her hip.

They walked to Courtney's car parked in a shady spot next to Happy House. She took the basket from Tally and swung it and the bags into the trunk.

Tally turned to her. "I wish you'd change your mind and come live with Eddie and me. We'd love to have you."

"I appreciate the offer, but I think Bobby and I should live on our own."

"But we're family now."

Courtney smiled. They *were* family now. Family. It seemed like such a foreign concept to her. She'd found out Tally and Eddie were her grandparents all from one antique ladies pocket watch and a single coded note. She reached up and wrapped her hand around the watch hanging from a gold chain around her neck.

Tally saw the movement, and a sad look briefly flashed across her face. She quickly replaced it with a genuine smile. "Well, if you're sure that's what you want."

The last thing Courtney wanted was to be a burden to Tally and Eddie. Her whole life she'd learned to take care of herself. She couldn't see changing that now. Besides, the four of them living in Tally's small cottage would be pure chaos. Well, anywhere her son was usually resulted in chaos, but she wouldn't change a thing. He was her whole life.

Courtney closed the trunk. "I'm sure. We'll still see you all the time, of course. You know, as long as you keep giving me shifts at Magic Cafe."

Tally's warm eyes twinkled with amusement. "I'm sure that could be arranged. We might need to hire another waitress though. I'm planning on teaching you even more about the business side of things."

Tally had been showing her some of the inner workings of running the cafe. She'd worked on inventory and closing the books each night so far.

"I don't know why you think I can learn all this. I didn't even finish high school. I just passed my high school equivalency test. What would I know about running the cafe?"

"Well, you'll know everything I teach you." Tally's voice was matter-of-fact.

"You're sure you want to teach *me*?"

"Of course, I want to teach you everything about the business." Tally reached out and touched her arm. "One day, Magic Cafe will be yours if you want it."

Courtney stared at her grandmother in

amazement. "Tally, I don't even know what to say."

"Say 'yes.'"

AJ pulled his sports car into the crushed shell parking lot of a place called Magic Cafe. He knew he shouldn't be stalling, but he was. A nice lunch and a couple of beers might fortify him for what he had to face later this afternoon.

He fit in nicely with the vacation crowd on Belle Island. Shorts, flip-flops, and a t-shirt from his favorite casino in Vegas. His father wouldn't approve of his dress, but then, when did his father approve of much of anything about him? Never had that been made more clear to him than his last lecture from his father, which had resulted in him having to make this trip.

"Hi. Table for one?" A pretty woman with blonde hair smiled at him, menus in hand. Her blue eyes sparkled as she efficiently juggled the menus as well as a tray full of water glasses.

"Yep, just me."

"Would you like to sit out by the beach?"

"Sure."

AJ followed the woman through the restaurant and back outside to the deck on the ocean side. She stopped and handed the tray to another waitress. He glanced at the other woman's name tag. Tereza. He tucked the name away. Never hurt to remember the names of pretty women. He hadn't gotten a chance to read the name tag of the cute blonde waitress he was dutifully following through the cafe. A mistake he planned on remedying at once.

Ceiling fans stirred the warm air, and tables were placed under a large wooden canopy. A row of tables lined the edge of the deck, right by the sand. Quite different than the trendy restaurants he usually frequented, but this one seemed to suit his mood now. Easy, friendly, no-frills. And no one knew him, so hopefully he wouldn't get into any trouble.

If he didn't bore himself to death.

"I'm Courtney, by the way." She handed him a menu.

Ah, she'd beaten him to the punch. Courtney smiled at him, and he returned it in kind with what he hoped was his famous dazzle-all-the-women smile.

She didn't look dazzled.

"I'll be back in a few minutes to take your order. Could I bring you a drink in the meantime?"

He figured it would be bad form to order two

beers at once. "I'll have a beer. Corona. In a bottle if you have it, no glass."

"Coming right up." She smiled as she turned away. The same smile she gave to every other customer she spoke to as she threaded her way through the tables. She stopped and said something to the other waitress. Tereza was tall and pretty with dark, almost-black hair and a quick smile. Maybe his smile would work on her...

Maybe he would be able to survive this banishment.

Courtney and Tereza sat at a table rolling silverware in napkins, enjoying a bit of a break after the lunch rush.

"I saw that good-looking guy you had at table six." Tereza grabbed another napkin.

"The one with brown hair and the well-practiced smile?"

Tereza laughed. "Yep, that's the one. Pretty sure I saw him checking out most of the women here at the cafe."

"Well, at least he's a good tipper." She shrugged. He'd been good-looking with chestnut brown eyes and dark brown hair in need of a cut. But he had an air about him as if he should have been wearing a business suit and eating at an expensive restaurant. Though, he certainly had enjoyed his grouper and hushpuppies. But then, who didn't love Tally's grouper and hushpuppies?

"Did you get moved?" Tereza efficiently rolled another napkin.

"I did. Well, everything is just dumped off at the apartment. I have to unpack everything, not that we have much." She frowned. "I really did love Happy House. I would have liked to just stay there. Tally and Eddie thought we should live somewhere nicer than the storage building, but I didn't mind. It was mine."

"Your new apartment complex looks nice. It has a great view of the bay from the courtyard."

"Yes, it's nice. I like that each unit is a cute little bungalow. There's a pool for Bobby to swim in and a playground. I hope he gets to meet some other kids to play with. Stevie, one of the boys he's in daycare with, lives there."

"Well, that sounds like it will work out great. Plus, it's only about a five-minute walk from here. You'll still be close. But wow, Tally sure wanted you and Bobby to move in with her and Eddie." Tereza grinned a knowing smile. "But I think Bobby might have been a little too much for that cottage."

"That's what I thought. Plus, Tally and Eddie just got married a few months ago. They need their privacy. Eddie even offered to buy us a cottage of our own, but I didn't want to take handouts like that. I pay my own way."

"But he's family. He just wanted to help you."

"I know, but… well, I want to make it on my own." She still didn't know how to trust all this luck she'd had wouldn't just disappear in an instant. "But now Tally says she wants to start training me—*me* —on the business side of Magic Cafe."

"I'm not surprised. She'll probably want you to run it one day."

"I can't run a place like this." She shook her head.

"Of course you can. Tally will teach you. You learn fast, I've seen it."

"I don't know… everything has changed so quickly."

Tereza reached over and squeezed her hand, a friendly gesture of support. "And you deserve every bit of good luck that's come your way."

AJ pulled his sports car in front of a decent-sized beach home. The house had large, expansive steps leading up to an oversized wooden door. After his father had texted him the address, he'd looked it up online. He knew it had a nice-sized swimming pool on the ocean side. The listing had said it had five bedrooms, a well-equipped kitchen, an overabundance of TVs and stereo systems, and a huge back deck with a great view of the sea.

He reached into the backseat, slung out his suitcase, and bounded up the front stairs. Might as well get it over with…

He knocked on the door and waited patiently. The door swung open, and Miss Chelsea gave him a welcoming smile. "Mr. Ashton, so nice to see you."

He walked in and kissed the woman on her cheek. "So I guess you got exiled, too."

"Now, Mr. Ashton, you know I wouldn't leave Miss Alice to fend for herself."

"I don't know what my grandmother would do without you."

"She won't ever have to find out."

AJ followed Miss Chelsea into the house. The woman never changed. She was his grandmother's housekeeper, cook, and companion. She'd worked for Granice—a name bestowed by her first grandchild, a mixture of Gran and Alice—for as long as AJ could remember.

He entered the main room and looked around in appreciation. Sunshine poured through the windows. The main floor was open with the kitchen at one side and comfortable-looking sofas and chairs scattered around the generously sized great room.

"There you are." Granice approached him and gave him a quick hug. "I'm so glad you decided to come stay with me for a while."

"It's not like I had much choice whatsoever, now did I?"

"Now, Ashton, you know your father only wants what's best for you."

"I'm pretty much old enough to know what's best for me all by myself."

"I could see that by your last escapade that got picked up in the papers." His grandmother pinned him with what he referred to as her trademarked I'm-on-to-you look. The one she'd used on him when his baseball had smashed through the window of her house when he was a boy. The one she'd used on him when he'd almost flunked out of college.

"It was just a minor skirmish. The media blew it all out of proportion." He shifted uneasily on his feet. That look of hers always made him squirm.

"That's the third time this year you've been in the paper for one of your so-called blown-out-of-proportion misadventures."

"I'm pretty old to be grounded." He was still annoyed with his father.

"Then act like it." She didn't pull any punches. Ever. "You know I love you, but you sure try my patience at times. It's time for you to settle down. Your father wants you to come back and work for his company, you know."

"I'm well aware of that fact. Have been since I was about five. I tried it, remember? How well did that work out?"

His grandmother stared at him for a moment. "Well, we'll talk about this later. Anyway, I'll enjoy your company while I'm here on vacation. It's a lovely island. Delbert was right. I'm glad he recommended it."

Delbert, AJ's older cousin, had followed in his own father's footsteps and now worked at Hamilton Hotels, the company AJ's uncle founded. Both his father and his uncle were powerful, competent businessmen.

Too bad only his uncle had gotten a son with the same characteristics.

"I've given you the master suite on the top floor. It's on the ocean side. I hope that's okay. I sure don't want to be going up that many flights of stairs. My room and Chelsea's are above this main floor. You're one up from that."

"Whatever works for you."

"Why don't you take your things on up and get settled?"

"Sounds good." He walked over to the stairway and climbed his way up to the top floor. The door to his room opened smoothly when nudged, and he stood on the threshold for a moment. A nice, king-sized bed was placed against one wall. An entire bank of windows ran across the side facing the sea, and daylight streamed into the room. He dropped his suitcase and walked over to the French door nestled between the long row of windows.

He pushed the door open and stepped out onto a large balcony. Stairs angled down on one end, all the way to the ground level. Perfect, he could come and go as he pleased, using these stairs instead of going through the main part of the house.

A few steps took him to the railing, and he leaned against the well-worn wood. A warm breeze blew in from the ocean. He ran his hands through his hair. He needed a haircut, but he'd purposely kept it long because it irritated his father. Not the most mature way to handle things, but he was tired of his father's interference in his life.

He turned from watching the waves roll in to check out the rest of the balcony. Two bar-height chairs and a table sat at one end. A couple of Adirondack chairs were grouped at the other end.

Nice. At least he'd have a place to escape to.

CHAPTER 2

The next day, AJ told his grandmother he was going out for a beach walk, but really he was headed for Magic Cafe again. He'd mapped it out and figured it was about a mile walk down the beach. A couple of midday beers and a good sandwich sounded like just what he needed.

He'd avoided his grandmother most of the morning, not wanting another lecture on his recent run-in with the law. She'd said he was free to come and go as he pleased as long as he stayed out of trouble.

What kind of trouble could he possibly get into here on Belle Island?

He strolled down the beach at the water's edge, watching families laugh and splash in the waves. His family had never taken a beach vacation… or any vacation for that matter. His father had taken him on one torturously long tour of Europe, but his father had been busy with business meetings most of the time. AJ continued down the beach until he spied the deck to Magic Cafe. He loped across the expanse of sand and stepped up to the cafe.

The same pretty blonde waitress—Courtney, right?—greeted him.

"Welcome back." She flashed him her welcoming smile, the exact same smile she gave to every customer.

"Thank you." AJ tried again with his own dazzle-smile. He could swear she almost rolled her eyes.

"Table outside again?"

"Yes, please." He followed her to the table and slid into his seat. "I'll take a beer again."

"Corona, bottle, no glass, right?"

Impressive. "Yes, that's right."

"I'll go get it."

He watched while she hurried across the distance, pausing for a moment to talk to Tereza, then disappeared behind a door. Tereza shot him a quick look then went back to wait on her customers.

He glanced around the restaurant. The workers bustled around but took time to chat with customers. A sign of good management. The menu had impressed him, too. From a good selection of fish, to a smattering of sandwiches, to an array of salads. The beer was icy cold, and he'd seen a list of good wines. Both times he'd been here, the place was packed. Maybe they should look into expanding…

He shook his head. This was not his problem.

Courtney returned soon with his ice-cold beer. "Do you know what you want?"

"I'll have the grouper again. Blackened this time."

"Blackened's my favorite." She jotted down his order.

"So, are you from here?" He handed her his menu.

"No, I just moved here a few months back. I plan on staying, though. I love it here."

"Seems like a nice place." He eyed her and did a quick calculation of his chances. "I don't suppose you'd like to show me around town? Maybe go out to eat? I'd like to find the local hot spots."

She laughed a delightful laugh that brought a spontaneous smile to his lips. "We don't really have what I'd call hot spots."

"Well, how about you just show me around town?"

She looked at him for a moment then shook her head. "I don't think so. I'm pretty busy these days."

He was losing his touch.

"But thanks for asking. I'm sure you'll sort out the town soon enough. It's not very big." She turned and walked away.

He sat and sipped his beer, wondering if his luck had all changed with his last mishap with the law.

"He asked you out?" Tereza stood pouring tea into an ice-filled glass.

"Yeah. But I said no, of course."

"Why 'of course'? Are you not allowed to date? Where is the rulebook that says you can't go out and have a good time?"

"I don't have time for that. I have this job and Bobby."

"When is the last time you've gone on a date?" Tereza's eyes narrowed.

"I... I can't remember. Years ago. Before I had Bobby."

"So, you're just afraid to, huh?"

"No, it's not that." Courtney paused filling a glass with ice. Was it that? Was she just afraid to try to go on a date again? She had to admit her ex, Kurt, had kind of soured her on dating. He'd been a horrible mistake. One she didn't want to repeat again.

"Why don't you go out with him? Have a nice dinner. Just be an adult and enjoy yourself."

"I already told him no." She finished filling up the glass with ice and reached for the pitcher of tea.

"Go back over and tell him you've changed your mind."

"I… I couldn't do that. Besides, look at him. He's… gorgeous. I'm not sure why he'd want to go out with me."

Tereza rolled her eyes. "Maybe because you're smart, funny, and have you looked in a mirror lately? The blonde hair agrees with you. So does your non-stressed-out look these days. Go back and say yes. A date would do you good."

Courtney walked out of the kitchen, delivered the iced tea to one of her tables, and eyed the man sitting by the beach. She didn't even know his name. She couldn't go out with someone if she didn't even know his name.

He waved to her, and she crossed over to him. "Another beer?"

"Yes, please. This one went down quickly."

She started to walk away to grab his beer but turned back to him. "I didn't catch your name."

"AJ."

"Okay, AJ, one beer coming up." She hurried back to the bar area and got his drink. Tereza walked past her and gave her a go-ahead-and-do-it look. Courtney sighed. Maybe she should go out. He seemed like a nice enough guy, even if he was a bit stuck on himself. She could go out this one time. One tiny step. She could meet him somewhere for dinner. Not even tell him where she lived. Just... a meeting with an acquaintance. That would work.

With a surge of sudden resolve, she spun around and hurried back to his table. "So, here's your beer. And would you still like me to show you around town?" Her words came out in a rush.

He gave her his now-familiar dazzle-the-women smile. "I would."

"I'm off tomorrow night. I could meet you at the gazebo at the end of Oak Street. I'll show you around, and we could grab dinner at The Lucky Duck."

"That sounds great."

"Six o'clock work?"

"Works for me."

She hurried off before one of the hundreds of

reasons why this was a bad idea could win their argument.

"Mom, have you seen my baseball glove?" Bobby called from his new bedroom. "Pops said he'd work with me some more on my catching."

Courtney set down the box of dishes she was unpacking and headed back to his room. "I think we packed up a box of all the sports equipment Eddie has gotten you." Which was a lot. Eddie was spoiling Bobby with all the things he'd never been able to do or get for his own son.

She walked over to the corner and shuffled some boxes around. "Here it is."

"Thanks, Mom. You're the best." Bobby rushed over and started to dig through the box. "You sure it's okay I go spend the night with Pops and Grams tomorrow night?" He frowned. "I'm kinda worried about leaving you home here by yourself."

She ruffled his curls. "Don't worry. I'll be fine. Besides, you'll have fun with Tally and Eddie. A special night with them."

"And Pops says he'll teach me to throw the baseball better because right now I'm the worst ever."

"All it takes is some practice."

Bobby's scowl clearly said he didn't believe her. "I'm gonna need me a *lot* of practice."

"Well, I'm sure Eddie will work with you, but right now, you need to go get ready for bed."

Bobby looked around his bedroom. "You think we can find my jammies in this mess?"

"I'll find your jammies. You go brush your teeth."

She opened a few more boxes until she found his pajamas. How had they acquired all this stuff? All their belongings in the world used to fit in the trunk of her car.

Well, most of it was because Tally and Eddie spoiled them with gifts. She needed to talk to her grandmother and have her cut back on the gift giving, but Tally seemed to get so much pleasure from giving them things. Courtney wasn't used to being given anything, and sometimes it was a bit overwhelming.

"Find them?"

"Yes, here you go." She held out the pajamas and went over to clear off his bed.

He pulled on the pajamas and climbed into bed. "I liked Happy House."

"I did, too."

"But Grams and Pops thought we should move, huh?"

"Well, it was really a storage building, even if it did have that room in the front for us."

"But I liked it." He let out a sigh too large and too long for such a young boy.

"But Stevie lives here. That will be nice, won't it? To have a friend here?"

"Yeah, I guess."

She didn't want to explain to a six-year-old boy that maybe Tally and Eddie needed a little space. They weren't used to the constant whirlwind of motion that surrounded Bobby.

"Well, you get to spend the night with them tomorrow."

"It's gonna be fun. Grams said I could make a fort out on her deck."

She smiled. She was sure Bobby would keep Tally and Eddie hopping until the moment he dropped off to sleep tomorrow night. "Okay. You'll have lots to do. But right now, it's sleep time." She reached over to turn out the light beside his bed.

"Momma?"

"Yes?"

"Can I have the light on tonight? I'm not a baby or anything, but… you know, in case I get up in the middle of the night. I don't want to trip on the boxes or something."

"That's probably a good idea." She switched the light back on. "Good night." She slowly walked out of his room and glanced back at him. He was already curled up with his eyes closed. He played hard, but when it was time for bed, he dropped like a stone.

She headed back to the kitchen, determined to finish unpacking it—mostly with kitchen supplies and dishes Tally had given her. Tally had insisted that she had way more than she needed.

She unwrapped the pretty white dishes with blue trim. The nicest dishes she'd ever owned. She clutched the watch hanging around her neck. "Thanks for looking out for us, Mom." She whispered the words into the air in the silent apartment.

Tally rinsed the last of the dinner dishes and put them in the dishwasher. She'd taken off early from Magic Cafe, and she and Eddie had eaten a quiet dinner at home.

Eddie walked into the kitchen. "One more." He handed her a plate.

She slipped it into the dishwasher and wiped her hands on the dish towel. He stood behind her, slipped his arms around her waist, and pressed a kiss to the side of her forehead.

"What's that for?"

"I'm just content."

"Ah, food will do that to a man."

"It has nothing to do with the dinner, though it was delicious." He turned her around and ran his finger along her cheek with the gentlest of touches.

Warmth spread through her. And pure, simple joy. She'd loved this man for so long, and it sometimes seemed like a fantasy that they'd found each other again. She reached up and touched his face covered with a day's worth of whiskers. "Let's go sit out on the deck. It's a beautiful night out."

"Sounds like a plan." Eddie grabbed an open bottle of wine and two glasses, and they went out to the deck. He poured their wine, and they sat in silence for a while, just enjoying the evening.

"What are you thinking about?" Eddie's low voice broke the silence.

"I'm thinking I wish we'd been able to get Courtney and Bobby to move in here with us. There's enough room. It would have made everything perfect."

"It's pretty perfect already." He smiled at her.

"But I think she just wanted to be on her own. She's an independent one, our granddaughter."

"But I would love having them here."

"I would, too. But we have to respect her decision. You'll still see her every day at Magic Cafe."

"I know, but that's not the same."

"Well, Bobby is coming to spend the night tomorrow."

"And I'm looking forward to it. I can't believe how much my life has changed in the last few months." Tally's heart swelled with happiness and a contentment she hadn't felt in many, many years.

"And my life, too. I wouldn't change a thing. Our life is perfect now." Eddie leaned over and kissed her again.

The silvery moonlight spilled down around them, convincing her she was the luckiest woman in the world.

CHAPTER 3

With Bobby spending the night with Tally and Eddie, the new apartment seemed unusually quiet. For some reason, Courtney hadn't told Tally she was going out on a date. Maybe because she was so self-conscious about it, maybe because she was afraid she'd made a mistake.

She stood and stared in her closet, wondering what she had to wear. Her clothes were limited. When she and Bobby had run away to hide from Kurt, they hadn't been able to take much. She didn't really need much, just clothes for work and some casual attire. She didn't think she had anything that counted as a dating outfit.

Courtney dug through a box of clothes she hadn't unpacked yet and found a simple flowing navy skirt. She dumped the contents of another box and found a white blouse. No, that would look like she was wearing a uniform. She sighed in frustration.

She wandered back over to the closet with its sparse contents, unsure what to do. She should just cancel. She could picture the conversation. "Hi, I'm canceling because I have nothing to wear." Not that she had his phone number to call and cancel.

Not that she even knew his last name.

What was she doing? She was a mother. She had responsibilities. She shouldn't be going out with a stranger.

Maybe she could just stand him up…

Courtney sighed again. No, she couldn't do that. Searching through the closet, she found a simple blouse with a tropical print. That would have to do. Not an outfit that would ever hit a trendy fashion magazine, but it was all she could come up with.

She dressed quickly then attempted to do something with her hair. She was letting it grow out again and return to its natural blonde color, after having cut it short and dyed it a mousy brown when she'd been hiding from Kurt. That was all past now, and she wanted her long blonde hair back. Right now, her hair was at that terrible in-between stage and impossible to do much with.

She looked in the mirror and fluffed her hair about in what she hoped looked like a deliberate, carefree style. She looked again. It just looked messy. With one last aggravated glare, she flipped off the light and left the mocking image in the mirror where it belonged.

AJ waiting patiently at the gazebo. He'd gotten there early. Any excuse to leave his grandmother's rental. Not that she'd brought up his behavior again nor his ongoing feud with his father. Could he call it a feud? Maybe it actually should be classified as a war. His father had made it very clear when he fired AJ that he was gravely disappointed in him.

But what else was new?

"Hi."

He'd been so lost in his thoughts, he hadn't even seen Courtney come up the sidewalk to the gazebo. "Hey."

"I thought we might walk along the boardwalk on the bayside? There's the pier down just a bit of a ways. Then we'll go down Oak Street, and I'll show you what's there. Then we'll pop into The Lucky Duck for dinner."

"Great." He looked at her appreciatively. She

had on a longish skirt that danced in the breeze, and the wind tossed her blonde hair around her face like some model with a fan turned on during a photoshoot. She wore minimal makeup on her tanned face. She looked healthy and wholesome and not anything like the women he usually dated. Yet, she intrigued him.

He followed her to the boardwalk, and they headed down toward the pier. "So, what brought you to come and live on Belle Island?"

"Uh…" A frown crossed her face, and she shrugged her delicate shoulders. "Chance, I guess you'd call it."

"As good a reason as any other."

They walked along the boardwalk, and she chatted to him about the birds on the shore and a large boat out on the bay owned by some regular to the town.

"We also have a legend about Lighthouse Point over on the gulf side of the island."

"What's that?" He enjoyed listening to her talk about the town. It was easy to tell she loved it here.

"According to the legend, a person can go out to the point, make a wish, and throw a shell in the ocean. Then the wish will come true."

"So, do you believe in the legend?" They

stopped at the end of the pier, watching a few men as they fished in the bay.

"I do. I've seen people's wishes come true."

He didn't think he believed in any folklore like that, but he'd let her live in her fantasy world. "So, is the legend the reason for *magic* in Magic Cafe and *luck* in The Lucky Duck?"

She leaned closer and spoke in a soft conspiratorial tone. "And so much more. A Wish and a Player is a sports bar here in town. There's Good Luck Mart and the Wishing Shop which is a souvenir store."

"The town people sure like to run with the theme, don't they?"

"They do, but I think it's kind of… quaint." She pushed a lock of hair out of her eyes. "I adore everything about this town. I'm lucky to have found it."

"There's that luck thing again." He grinned at her. He seemed to be unable to stop grinning this evening.

Her face broke into a delighted smile, not the courteous one she gave to all her customers. "Don't knock it. You should make your own wish out at Lighthouse Point."

He doubted that would ever happen. Not in a million years.

∾

Courtney hated to admit that maybe Tereza had been right. She was having a good time with this AJ no-last-name fella.

She *really* should ask him his full name at some point…

But she was enjoying their easy banter and the freedom from responsibilities, if only for one short night. It was easy to walk and talk about the town. He was easy to talk to and seemed genuinely interested in the tidbits she told him. They headed into The Lucky Duck after their stroll along Oak Street.

She hadn't been to The Lucky Duck. It's not like she had much downtime to go out to eat. But Tally had introduced her to the owner, Will, when he'd come to Magic Cafe. Will stood behind the bar, chatting with a customer. He waved when they walked in. "Take a seat anywhere."

They took a table toward the back of the tavern. Will came over with menus and a welcoming smile. "Courtney, right? Tally's granddaughter?"

"That's right."

"Glad you came in. Can I get you something to drink? My special is a Basil-Motonic."

"I don't know what that is, but that sounds fine," AJ said.

"I'm always concocting some kind of special drink, but the Basil-Motonic seems to be the customer favorite."

"I'll try one too. I think?" She was skeptical, but this whole night was an adventure, why not try some new drink?

"You'll love it. I promise. If not, I'll get you something else." Will walked away to get their drinks.

"Does everyone know everyone here on Belle Island?" AJ leaned back in his chair, relaxed and at ease.

She didn't know how he could be so relaxed because she realized she was going to have to carry on a normal adult conversation with him now that they were seated across from each other. No more just easily pointing out things around the town as they walked.

This dinner conversation probably wouldn't be anything like her normal ones with Bobby. Topics such as what Stevie, Mikey, and Billy had said at childcare that day. She heard about it in excruciating detail each night. Young boy brains were amazing things, and what they came up with amused her. Or they'd talk about why the sky was blue. Or why Bobby had to eat his vegetables.

What was she thinking before her thoughts trailed to Bobby? Oh, yes. Adult conversation. "So, are you visiting the island for long?" *That should work, right? A benign question, but showing interest in him.*

"I'm here for about a month. Maybe longer. Maybe shorter if I can arrange it. I... ah, I'm staying with my grandmother. She's rented a house here on the island. Supposed to stay for the month, but... well, I'd rather not."

"So you'll just have her stay here alone?"

"Oh, she won't be alone. She has Miss Chelsea with her. Miss Chelsea is kind of her companion-slash-housekeeper-slash-cook."

"So you might have to get back to work before the month is over?"

"No... it's not that." He shifted in his chair, his previous ease shattered. "I'm... kind of between jobs right now."

Ah, that was rough. Courtney had lived in fear of losing the countless jobs she'd had. She always made sure she found a job—any kind of job—if she ever lost one. She had to have income to support Bobby. He was her number one responsibility.

Though, AJ probably looked for some kind of

high-powered job. He seemed the type. Those kinds of jobs were probably harder to get and took longer to find.

AJ wasn't about to tell Courtney his job troubles. How he'd had the job with his father's company and screwed it up. That had been two years ago, and he hadn't worked a day since. He'd half-heartedly tried to find work, but not very hard. He had a trust fund to tide him over. He'd even convinced himself he liked his carefree life, invited to the best parties in New York and Los Angeles. Running with a fast crowd. Hopping over to Europe for different festivals. It was a good life.

Well, it had been until he'd been with some friends who had gotten themselves arrested on their last trip to Europe. Some expensive lawyers had smoothed it over, and they'd all come home safely, but it had, of course, hit all the papers.

Then his father had grounded him to the island. That's the only way to look at this exile. Go to the island with his grandmother and stay out of the news or lose access to his trust fund. But he wasn't about to tell Courtney *that* either.

"I hope you can find work soon. I'm sure it's

worrisome to be out of a job."

"I'm sure something will turn up." Of course, he'd been saying that for a couple of years now, much to his father's disgust. But then, he kind of liked annoying his father, so there was that.

Will delivered their beverages. AJ took a sip of the specialty drink. Then another. It tasted like a mix between a mojito and a gin and tonic. "This is great, Will."

Will grinned and waited for Courtney to try hers.

She took a sip and her eyes widened. "Oh, this is good. I wasn't sure." She took another good sip.

AJ smiled at her enthusiasm.

"Great. Glad you like them. Always like to hear my customers say they like my drinks." A self-satisfied look crossed Will's face. "So, can I take your dinner order?"

They ordered burgers and fries, and Will headed back to the bar.

"I've heard their burgers are great here." Courtney sat up straight in her chair, tense, looking a bit out of sorts.

He wasn't sure what he'd done to cause that. They'd been having a great time, he thought, walking around the town. "You haven't been to The Lucky Duck before?"

"No, I don't get out much." She looked like she was going to say more, bit her bottom lip, then remained quiet.

"Well, glad you decided to come out with me tonight and show me around." AJ took another sip of the delicious drink then leaned back in his chair, stretching out his legs. He was glad she'd said yes. He was having a good time, which surprised him. It was just a simple evening of walking along the bay and browsing Oak Street, but he'd enjoyed her company.

She seemed like a really nice person and not worried about what others thought, which was a refreshing change. She seemed unconcerned with wearing the newest trend in clothes whether it looked ridiculous on someone or not. He'd seen her cell phone... and he'd probably gotten six versions of cell phones himself since hers had been manufactured.

All this about Courtney oddly reassured him. What did they call this type of person? Down-to-earth, wasn't it? Or unpretentious. Anyway, he planned to ask her out again, and that surprised him too. He rarely dated the same woman more than once. He preferred to just...

What?

Not get tied down. No responsibilities. Because

that way he couldn't disappoint them.

"You okay?"

"What?" He looked up at Courtney.

"You looked lost in thought."

"I guess I was." His leg bumped against hers. "Oops, sorry." He angled his legs away from hers and grabbed his drink, taking a long refreshing swallow sure to wash away his bouncing thoughts.

It was obvious he'd drifted off, lost in his own thoughts. Courtney couldn't even keep him interested in her while they waited for their dinner. She was a dating flop, that's all there was to it. She knew this had been a mistake. Maybe she could go to the ladies room and then come back and act like she'd gotten called away.

Where is your backbone, woman?

She took a deep breath and tried again with the whole dating conversation thing. "So, where are you from?"

"I grew up near Washington, DC. Mostly. I went to a boarding school, so I was gone most of the time."

"I can't even imagine that."

"Where's your family from?"

She noticed he quickly sidestepped talking about his family. His eyes almost looked like he was truly interested in her answer. But she knew better. She wasn't really his type.

And she didn't know how to answer his question. Well, Tally and Eddie were here. Her only family now. She'd leave it at that. "My grandparents live here." She didn't need to get into the fact her other grandmother had raised her and loathed every minute of it. She'd never let Courtney forget her mother had died in childbirth having her. It was Courtney's fault that her grandmother's only daughter was dead.

She also didn't think a boarding school-raised man would understand what it had been like to be on her own since she turned eighteen.

At least until she'd found Tally.

Will brought their dinners, and she carefully steered the conversation to the weather and the Lighthouse festival coming up soon. Safe topics. She considered telling him about Bobby, but the whole story of Bobby and her ex and… well, it's not like she was going out with AJ again. She wasn't even in his league. *Boarding school.* She hadn't even finished high school and had to take the equivalency test to even get a high school diploma.

Jeepers. Who really goes to boarding school?

CHAPTER 4

The next morning, Tereza helped Courtney
set up for the breakfast crowd.

"So, how was your date?" Tereza set out a tray
of clean coffee mugs.

"It was… fine."

"Fine? That's all I get?"

"It was okay. One thing I'm sure of, though.
We're from different worlds. He went to *boarding
school*, for Pete's sake. I think he was just looking to
kill some time while he's here on vacation. I
probably won't see him again."

"Don't be so sure." Tereza elbowed her and
bobbed her head toward the entrance.

Courtney turned and saw him. AJ still-without-
a-last-name because she'd forgotten to ask him. He
looked like he'd stepped out of a magazine. Rich

casual. A nice t-shirt—not like the well-washed, beat-up ones she owned—shorts, leather sandals, and sunglasses that probably cost more than a week of her wages.

Okay, she'd give him handsome. Very handsome.

He waved to her, and she made her way over to him. "Good morning."

"Morning. I thought I'd try out breakfast here."

"I'll show you to a table." She dropped the menu, not sure why she was so jumpy, and bent to pick it up. He reached for it at the same time, and their hands touched. She jerked her hand back.

AJ rescued the menu and followed her to the table.

"Do you want coffee?" He was just like any other customer. Get him a drink. Get his order. Quit being a nervous ninny.

"I do. Black. Thanks."

She hurried off to get the coffee, annoyed with herself for being nervous. He'd just come in for food. They'd had their date. It hadn't been anything spectacular, right? He'd asked to walk her home, but she'd said no. The place was a disaster of boxes and things thrown everywhere.

She filled his mug and returned to the table,

positive she could act like a rational human being now.

He smiled that dazzle-smile of his at her as she set his mug down, and she almost dumped the hot liquid all over him. Which was silly, because she was sure that was his charm-the-ladies smile.

"Do you know what you want?"

"Bacon, eggs—fried—and toast."

"I'll put your order in." She rushed away before he had a chance to say another word.

"I still want to hear about your date. He obviously had a good time if he's back here this morning." Tereza passed by her on the way to wait on a new table of customers.

"Or he's hungry." She tossed the words back over her shoulder as she headed into the kitchen.

Eventually, she had no choice but to bring him his breakfast when it was up. She'd considered asking Tereza to bring it to him, but that seemed like a cowardly thing to do. She didn't know why he was putting her so off-kilter.

"Here you go." She set his food on the table.

"Do you have time to sit for a moment?"

"I—I better not."

"Just a moment."

"Okay." She slid into the seat across from him, trying valiantly to seem nonchalant.

"So, I had a good time last night." He leaned forward toward her. "I... well, I wondered if you'd go out with me again."

"Are you sure?" The words just slipped out.

AJ laughed a delighted chuckle. "I'm sure."

"Okay."

"Okay, we can go out again?" He cocked his head.

"Yes." Why had she said yes? Did she want to go out again? Hadn't she just gone out that one time so she could say she'd finally had a date again?

"Great. What works for you? My schedule is pretty open."

"Momma." Bobby came flying through the restaurant and launched himself into her arms.

She wrapped him in a hug. "Hey, kiddo. Did you have a good time with Tally and Eddie?"

"The best ever. But Pops brought me here 'cause I missed you." Bobby turned to AJ. "Hi. I'm Bobby. Who are you?"

She turned her attention to AJ and paused. She recognized that look in his eyes.

Surprise. Displeasure. The look that adults who don't like kids show when a child comes into their space.

She tightened her arm around Bobby. "Bobby,

this is Mr… I'm sorry. I don't even know your last name."

"Hamilton." A stunned look still clung to his face.

"Mr. Hamilton," she continued. "AJ, this is my son, Bobby."

"Nice to meet you, Mr. Hamilton." Bobby was all correct manners as he'd been taught.

"I… uh… yes."

So maybe AJ hadn't been taught quite as well as Bobby.

"I mean, good to meet you, too." AJ recovered. Slightly.

"Bobby, why don't you go into the kitchen and see if they have any cinnamon rolls from The Sweet Shoppe. I'll be right in."

"Okay, I bet Pops might want one, too." He slipped out of her arms and skipped off in the direction of the kitchen.

She turned to AJ and tilted her head to the side. Daring him with a look she hoped said now-ask-me-out.

"I…" AJ raked his hand through his hair, his eyes still holding a deer-in-the-headlights look. "I didn't know you had a kid."

"Obviously." She stood. "Don't worry about it. We'll pretend you didn't ask me out again. I can see it plainly on your face. You don't want to go out with a woman who's a package deal. And I am. Bobby and I. We only had each other for years. And he's a great kid, by the way. I'll have Tereza bring you more hot coffee. Goodbye, Mr. Hamilton." She turned away, head held high and shoulders straight in what she hoped was a good impression of washing her hands of him. The last thing she needed in her life was a man who was afraid of kids. Why she'd thought she was ready to date again remained a mystery. She wasn't ready. Not by a long shot.

Tereza stopped her at the kitchen door. "Well, that was pretty obvious, wasn't it?"

"The look of pure terror on AJ's face when Bobby came up to me?"

"I wanted to laugh, it was so obvious. Kids scare some men."

"Or some men are just players. He'd just asked me out again. He obviously rued that decision after he met Bobby."

"I'm sorry, Courtney. I just thought you could have some fun with him. Go out a few times. Relax."

"I really don't have time for that kind of nonsense anyway." She pushed her way into the kitchen, unsure why she felt a bit saddened and mad at herself for feeling that way. It had been one night. Even if he had asked her out again. It wasn't like some big breakup. She shook her head at her own craziness.

Men. They thought women were the complicated ones. Ha. Not even.

Tally, Julie, and Susan sat at The Sweet Shoppe, sipping on sweet tea and nibbling on apricot scones. Julie, as usual, kept glancing around the shop to make sure all her customers were taken care of.

"I heard Courtney had a date last night." Susan leaned forward.

"She what?" Tally frowned. That couldn't be right. "I don't think so. I mean, she didn't say anything. Eddie and I did have Bobby over to spend the night last night."

"Jamie heard it from Will. I swear my son hears more about what's going on around here than I do." Susan sighed. "Anyway, Will said Courtney was in The Lucky Duck with some tall, dark stranger."

"I… I can't imagine why she wouldn't have said something. I mean, I'm pretty sure she hasn't had a date since she's been here. But then, she's either working or taking care of Bobby." Tally stirred her tea even though it didn't need stirring. Why would Courtney have kept it a secret? Who had she gone out with?

"I wouldn't worry about it. Maybe it was just some spur-of-the-moment thing." Julie reached for a scone.

"Maybe." Tally wracked her mind, trying to think of anyone who Courtney could be going out with. She didn't know if her feelings were hurt because Courtney hadn't said anything or if she was worried Courtney was keeping secrets. Of course, her granddaughter was entitled to her privacy, but she wished Courtney would share things like this with her. Well, the girl would talk to her when she felt the time was right. Or not.

Tally turned to Susan. "So, how are things with Adam? Still enjoying that married life?"

"I am. I swear, I'm so lucky." Susan's face beamed when she talked about her husband. "But we're getting a bit worried about his mother. Her Alzheimer's is progressing."

"I saw Mary out walking Stormy on the beach the other day." Tally reached for one of Julie's delicious cinnamon rolls. "She was alone."

"We don't want to say she can't go out walking her dog… but I wish she'd take someone with her each time."

"I'm sure it's hard on her and hard on you two." Julie glanced around the shop again, caught the waitress's eye, and nodded toward a table near the window. The waitress hurried over to the table.

"It is. It's a horrible disease. We want her to have as independent a life as possible while she can. But it's hard."

"Well, at least she has you two to take care of her," Tally said. "It's good she lives with you ."

"I feel like we have a village watching over her here on Belle Island. Dorothy and Mary have become great friends, and when Dorothy isn't working the front desk at the inn for us, she's usually off knitting somewhere with Mary. And they have their knitting group, too. Lots of people watch over Mary."

Tally reached over and squeezed Susan's hand. "We all have come to love Mary. We'll help in any way we can. I thought I'd pop over and see if she wanted to take Stormy on a walk this afternoon."

"That would be wonderful. I'm sure she'd like that. I know Adam feels better if someone goes with her on her walks."

Tally turned to Julie who was scanning the shop again. "Quit watching the shop and relax for a bit." Though, Tally knew she did the same thing at Magic Cafe. It was never truly out of her mind.

"Sorry. Occupational hazard."

"Looks like you've been doing a good business this summer."

"We have. And quite a few catering gigs too. The Montgomerys actually asked me to cater one of their parties in a couple of weeks. I really wanted to say no after last time."

"You mean when they accused you of stealing from them?" Susan rolled her eyes.

"Exactly." Julie shrugged. "But I do usually get more business from their parties, so it was hard to turn it down."

"Well, Cindy seems to think Camille is softening." Susan leaned forward. "Ever since Cindy went to work at The Hamilton in Sarasota after marrying my Jamie, she's run into Camille quite a lot. They seem to have found some kind of common footing... or at least a truce."

"I'll believe it when I see it." Julie's eyebrows rose.

Their conversation turned to the Lighthouse festival at the end of the month. Tally sat and listened to her friends chatter about who was doing what for the festival this year. She loved times like this with them. Talking about everything and nothing.

Her life was so full these days. Good friends. A

second chance with her wonderful husband… and a family. Courtney and Bobby. Life didn't get much better than this.

AJ was thankful he and Courtney hadn't really firmed up any plans to go out again. The last thing he wanted was to date a woman with a kid. Maybe that made him shallow and callous, but he was who he was.

Now he was going to have to find a new place to go eat his meals if he didn't want to run into Courtney again. Though, he'd miss Magic Cafe's grouper and hushpuppies…

He walked down from his upper-level room where he'd been resting—okay, hiding out for the afternoon—and into the great room on the main level. His grandmother sat on an overstuffed chair, reading the paper. A real paper. He didn't know anyone who still did that except her.

She looked up and smiled at him. "Hi, dear. There's some tea in the fridge if you'd like some."

AJ walked into the kitchen. For a moment, he debated on getting a beer instead but decided his grandmother would prefer he drink the tea. He searched for the cabinet with the glasses and poured himself a tall glass of tea. Clutching the cold glass, he went back in and sat on a chair across from his grandmother. He'd been feeling guilty he hadn't spent much time with her.

"Do you have any plans for later today?" She folded her paper and set it on an end table beside her.

"I thought I might go to the beach. I want to go see the lighthouse."

"I've heard it's very pretty."

"The town has a silly legend about it. If you go to Lighthouse Point, make a wish, and toss a shell into the sea, your wish will come true."

"Do you think there's any truth to it?" Granice tossed him an amused look.

"Not one bit." He took a swallow of his tea.

"Well, it's a nice legend anyway."

"I guess. If a person believes in that kind of nonsense."

"Will you be here for dinner tonight?"

"I think I'll eat in town if that's okay with you."

"You can come and go as you please, Ashton. You're not in prison."

"If you say so." He quickly corrected himself. "Not that I mind spending time with you, of course."

"Of course. You always were a sweet talker." Her

eyes twinkled. "Oh, but I did make plans for us for tomorrow night. I hope that's okay."

"Sure, what plans?"

"Delbert and his girlfriend, Camille, are going to meet us for dinner."

He hadn't seen his cousin Delbert in a while. It might be nice to catch up with him, and Camille was always entertaining in her own way.

"That sounds good."

"Great. We're meeting them at a place called Magic Cafe. Seven o'clock."

He set his glass down with a clatter.

Perfect. Just perfect.

CHAPTER 5

AJ walked along the beach until the lighthouse grew larger and larger as he approached. A mother stood at the water's edge, watching her little girl splashing in the waves. A lone runner ran up to him and nodded as he passed in the curious ritual strangers have when they pass each other on the beach.

As he walked along, he carried on a running conversation in his mind with his father. Listing his grievances and telling the man how outrageous he was. It didn't seem to help. He noticed he was walking with clenched fists. Weren't beach walks supposed to relax a person? He slowly and deliberately opened his hands.

In the distance, he saw two women walking a

small dog. A young boy chased around them, racing to the water's edge and back.

As they got closer, AJ frowned. That looked a lot like Courtney's boy, but that would be too much of a coincidence. It was a small island, but not that small.

He considered turning around, just in case, but he'd set his sights on getting to the lighthouse. But he could be flexible, the lighthouse would be there tomorrow. He paused.

"Hey, Mr. Hamilton." The boy raced up to him. "Hi there. Remember me? I'm Bobby. You like to play on the beach, too? I'm here with Grams and Miss Mary. We're taking Stormy for a walk."

The two older women approached with the dog.

"Grams, this is Mr. Hamilton."

"Nice to meet you." The woman greeted him with a genuine smile that filled her eyes with warmth.

"And this is Miss Mary." The boy dropped to his knees by the dog. "And this is Stormy. Isn't he great? I want a dog, but Momma says I can't have one. Not until I'm older and more 'sponsible."

The other woman, Miss Mary, smiled.

"Nice to meet both of you."

"I met Mr. Hamilton at Magic Cafe when Pops

took me there this morning. Momma introduced me to him. Magic Cafe is Grams' restaurant."

AJ reeled from all the information being thrown at him.

The first woman reached out her hand. "I'm Tally. As Bobby said, I own Magic Cafe where Courtney works."

He shook her hand, feeling a bit dazed.

"And Miss Mary's son married Miss Susan and Miss Susan owns Belle Island Inn." Bobby leapt up.

Tally laughed. "He's a wealth of information, isn't he?"

"He is." AJ glanced around, seeking a place to escape.

Nothing but open beach.

"Well, we should keep going on our walk." Tally took Bobby's hand. "It appears neither Stormy nor Bobby are tired out yet."

The trio headed down the beach, and he continued toward the lighthouse, trying to sort out all the information Bobby had thrown at him. But what did it matter? He'd probably not see Courtney again. She'd been working day shifts before when he'd seen her at Magic Cafe. Hopefully, she wouldn't be working tomorrow evening. Holding onto that hope firmly, he continued down the beach.

When he got to the point, he stood by the lighthouse, staring out at the sea. A lazy breeze cooled him, and birds darted along the water's edge. He took a deep breath of the clean air, pushing thoughts of his father firmly away from conscious thought. He dropped to the sand and sat staring at the waves. Gradually, a peace settled over him. He stretched out his legs and let the afternoon sun warm his skin. In a slow, lazy motion, he picked up a handful of sand and watched while it shifted through his fingers until his hand was empty and he was staring down at the lifelines creasing his palms. He wondered what they said about his life. A blue heron landed awkwardly at the water's edge. It gave him a solemn look for a moment before wandering on down the beach.

He watched while one rogue wave rushed toward him, almost hitting his feet. A lone shell tumbled in the water then rested right in front of him, glistening with drops of seawater. He ignored it.

Standing, he brushed the sand from his shorts. He started to leave but then turned around. He reached down, scooped up the shell, and tossed it in a perfect arc into the water.

Without making a wish, of course.

After their walk, Tally followed Bobby up the steps to Magic Cafe and over to where Courtney was setting things up for the evening crowd.

"Momma, I had the bestest walk with Grams and Miss Mary. They let me have the leash some, too. *Grams* thinks I'm 'sponsible."

"I'm glad you had a good time." Courtney hugged Bobby.

"And guess what? We saw your friend Mr. Hamilton."

"He's... ah... he's not my friend. He's just a... customer."

A blush crept over Courtney's cheeks. Tally watched her carefully. Was this Hamilton the man who she'd gone out with?

"Eddie is inside waiting for you. He said you two were going for burgers and ice cream tonight." Courtney deftly changed the subject.

"Yep. It's guys' night out." Bobby puffed out his chest. "I'm a guy, you know. A 'sponsible one. I'm probably 'sponsible enough for my own dog."

"Bobby, we've talked about it. Things are a little too crazy in our lives now for a dog."

He let out a long sigh. "But I'd take care of him. I'd do everything."

59

"Go find Eddie. I need to get back to work. Have fun on your guys' night out."

"I will," Bobby called back over his shoulder as he hurried off to find Eddie.

"That walk didn't wear him down a bit." Tally shook her head. "He has boundless energy."

"Always," Courtney agreed.

"So, do you know much about this Hamilton guy? I wonder if he's related to Delbert Hamilton?"

Courtney frowned. "Do you think so? He didn't say anything about that."

"When you went out with him?" Tally slipped it in as casually as she could.

Courtney looked at her and shook her head. "Nothing is secret here on Belle Island, is it?"

"I don't know why you thought it had to be a secret."

"Oh, I didn't really. I just… I didn't want to make a big deal out of it. It was more like I was just showing him around town."

"I see. So, are you showing him around town again?"

Courtney shook her head. "Nope. He asked me out… but did a fancy backtrack when he found out about Bobby. I don't have time for dating anyway. I've got plenty to keep me busy with Magic Cafe and Bobby."

"Never hurts to take some time for yourself." She was one to talk. Eddie had been begging her to go away with him if only for a long weekend, but she kept saying she needed to be here to run Magic Cafe.

"Well, if I did want to go out with someone again, it certainly wouldn't be Mr. Hamilton."

Tally thought Courtney protested a little too vehemently, but then if the man had been scared off by one small boy, he definitely wouldn't be a good match for Courtney.

So, if Courtney was ready to date again… Tally wondered who she could set her up with.

CHAPTER 6

A J drove his grandmother to Magic Cafe. They arrived precisely at six o'clock. His grandmother hated being late, while he'd developed the habit of being fashionably late. It's just what was done in the circles he ran in these days. But Granice would never allow them to be late. He opened the door for her, and they walked inside. His glance darted around, hoping he wouldn't find Courtney here.

So far, so good.

Tereza came up to them. "Hello. Table for two?"

"No, we're meeting two more." AJ searched the cafe for his cousin.

Just then, the door to the restaurant popped open, and Delbert and Camille entered.

"Ashton, so nice to see you." Camille grabbed his hands and kissed first one cheek and then the other. "I was so surprised to hear from Delbert that you were staying here on Belle Island. And he said you were here for a month. Whatever for?"

"Camille, darlin', let the man be." His cousin reached out his hand. "Nice to see you, AJ."

Finally, someone in the family who called him by his preferred nickname. Delbert was actually the only one in his family who did. "Delbert. It's been a while."

"I think we last saw him in New York City. Remember, we went out to all those parties? I do love it when you take me to New York to check on The Hamilton there." Camille smoothed her skirt. "We should do it again, soon, shouldn't we? Ashton, you'd like to do that again, wouldn't you?"

He didn't think she was really waiting for an answer. It was more a statement than a question.

His cousin walked over and kissed their grandmother. "Granice, it's great to see you. I'm glad you decided to come vacation on the island."

"I'm glad you suggested it. I love it here. It's a cute little town."

"Would you like to sit inside or out?" Tereza stood with menus in hand, but he didn't miss the slightly disapproving look she was trying to hide from him.

"Outside would be nice, dear," Granice answered for all of them.

A quick look of displeasure crossed Camille's face. "It's awfully muggy out."

"Oh, I think it will be fine. See, they have ceiling fans out there." Granice followed Tereza.

AJ had kind of hoped they'd eat inside, too, on the off chance Courtney was working. It seemed like she usually worked the outside tables, so inside would be… safer.

He followed his group to a nice table with a wonderful view of the beach. Though, he was more interested in looking around to make sure Courtney wasn't there.

Tereza watched him for a moment. "She's in the kitchen."

"What? I…"

"Don't worry. I'll be your waitress."

He didn't know whether he was grateful or disappointed Tereza would be their waitress. He didn't really want to run into Courtney, did he?

Then he saw her. She pushed her way out of the kitchen with a full tray and cheerful smile as she headed for a nearby table. She froze as she saw him, and the tray shook slightly in her hands. She recovered quickly, steadied the tray, and turned her back on him to serve the food to her customers.

He slid into a chair beside his grandmother but still watched Courtney from the corner of his eye.

"So, shall we get a bottle of wine? Tally has a small but good wine list." Delbert opened the menu.

"Very small." Camille set the wine list down dismissively.

"That sounds wonderful, Delbert." Granice put her napkin in her lap. "You choose for us."

"I think I'll stick with beer." He wondered how many beers he could have before Granice gave him one of her famous disapproving looks.

Delbert ordered the wine, and AJ ordered his beer. Courtney was noticeably gone from the floor of the restaurant… not that he actually, well, *noticed*.

"Ashton, you must come into Sarasota for the evening. As you've probably found out, there is really nothing to do on Belle Island and very limited places to go out to eat. There's a new club that opened in Sarasota. Do say you'll come into town and go to it. I'd love to have someone interesting to go with."

"Hey, what about me?" Delbert smiled indulgently at Camille.

"Oh, honey, you know what I mean." Camille turned back to AJ. "We're staying at The Hamilton in Sarasota this week. We have a marvelous suite there. You heard Delbert bought a hotel there and converted it to a Hamilton Hotel, didn't you?"

"I did."

"It's very… well, he had a new woman working on the remodel, and it's not quite like the other Hamilton Hotels."

"It's better." Delbert flashed a self-confident smile. "Not quite as stuffy. Fits in well with the more casual atmosphere in Florida."

"I still say your daddy isn't going to be pleased when he comes and sees it."

"But *I'm* pleased with it."

Camille shook her head. "Anyway, you must come to town. Say you will."

"I'll check my schedule." Not that he had anything on his schedule, and a trip to town and a night out at a trendy club was just what he was used to doing with his evenings. So, why didn't it sound that appealing to him?

"In a few weeks, we're going to be staying at my family's house on the island. Mama is coming down from Comfort Crossing. We've been renting out the family house here, which I'm not pleased with.

67

Strangers in our home. But we didn't use it much. It just seemed… practical… to rent it out."

He was pretty sure practical was the last word he'd use to describe Camille.

"Anyway, I'm planning a party there. You'll come, won't you? It will be so much fun." As almost an afterthought, she turned to Granice. "Oh, you should come, too."

"We'd love to, dear."

And just like that Granice had decided his schedule. Okay, then.

He took a grateful swig of his beer when Tereza handed it to him and then pretended not to search the restaurant for signs of Courtney.

Courtney hid out in the kitchen as much as possible. Tereza delivered food to some of her tables for her. She just wanted to avoid AJ. That wasn't too much to ask.

Tally walked into the kitchen. "What's up with Tereza serving your table? You feeling okay?"

"I'm fine. I'm just… an idiot." She shrugged. "I'm trying to avoid AJ, but it's really not fair of me to have Tereza serve my tables." She dried her hands on her apron. "I'm going out there right now. You're right. I shouldn't be hiding."

Tally didn't say a word but watched as Courtney picked up a pitcher of water.

Courtney marched out into the restaurant and over to one of her tables, filling their glasses with ice water and chatting with them. She deliberately avoided looking over at AJ. Pretty much. She did sneak a quick glance or two.

He seemed to be having a fabulous time. Laughing with Camille Montgomery and Delbert Hamilton, and she assumed the older lady must be his grandmother who he was staying with. She hadn't quite figured it all out, but if AJ's last name was Hamilton and Delbert's last name was Hamilton, they must be related in some way.

She looked over and saw Tereza was swamped by an eight-top table Tally had just seated. Mr. Hamilton was trying to get Tereza's attention. Courtney took a deep breath and walked over to see what Mr. Hamilton needed.

"Mr. Hamilton, Tereza is busy with a new table, can I help you?" She looked directly at Delbert Hamilton and avoided AJ, but not before catching the look of surprise in his eyes.

"I was wondering if we could get another bottle of wine."

"I can get that for you." She looked quickly at the label of the empty bottle.

"I'd appreciate that."

"Granice, AJ, this is Courtney. She's Tally's granddaughter. Tally owns Magic Cafe. Don't know if you know all that info about the island." Mr. Hamilton made the introductions. "Courtney, this is my cousin, AJ, and my grandmother, Mrs. Hamilton.

"I… uh… nice to meet you."

AJ leaned back in his chair as if this meeting wasn't a bit awkward. "Courtney and I have met. We're… friends." He eyed her as if daring her to say more.

"Yes, he's been in here a few times." She hurriedly cleared the table of a handful of empty dishes, trying not to spill them. "I'll be back with your wine."

She could almost feel AJ's eyes boring into her back as she walked away.

"AJ, so you know her?" Camille frowned and tossed her long, perfectly curled hair behind her shoulder. "She moved to town just a while ago. She has this incredibly out-of-control son, too."

"Camille, don't be like that. Bobby's a good kid. He's just a boy-boy. A very cute and *active* boy." Delbert smiled. "I like him."

"He ran me over on the beach, and I ruined a good pair of slacks." Camille shook her head. "He's a monster."

"He's just a normal little six-year-old boy," Delbert insisted.

Weirdly, and for no reason AJ could discern, he wanted to defend Bobby, too. Which was strange, because he didn't even know the kid. But Delbert seemed to be doing a good job of defending the boy on his own.

AJ watched the exchange between Camille and his cousin. They seemed like such different people, but Delbert obviously adored Camille. Camille was... well, she'd always been *Camille*. Full of opinions of others and herself. He liked her well enough, she was fun, but he certainly could never have dated her. She was too high-maintenance for his tastes.

Though she did always seem to find out about the best parties...

"Anyway, so you'll come into town this week, right? How about Friday? I'm sure Delbert can make reservations at the club, right, honey?"

"I can try."

"Then it's all settled. We'll all go out on Friday. You can meet us at the hotel at, say, eight?"

Camille didn't really wait for anyone to agree. He didn't have any other plans, so he decided he might as well say yes. "That sounds fine." He gave his half-hearted reply while he watched for Courtney's return, but Tereza came out with their new bottle of wine.

"Here's your wine. Sorry for the wait. Would you like to see the dessert menu?" Tereza opened the wine.

"Yes, I'd love to see it." Granice smiled at Tereza. "A spot of something sweet after that delicious meal sounds wonderful."

AJ didn't want dessert… didn't want *anyone* to order dessert. He just wanted to head out. But it seemed he was trapped here for a bit longer. "Tereza, I'll have another beer, please."

CHAPTER 7

The next day, AJ escaped to the beach again. He'd begun to like his new daily routine of just wandering along the shoreline. He'd never thought that would be something he'd do, but its peacefulness appealed to him. It was almost like doing *nothing*, which was something that he never did. Ever.

He headed away from Lighthouse Point this time. Shoes in hand, he walked in the water, mindlessly picking up an occasional seashell. The bright sun warmed his cheeks, and he was glad he'd remembered his sunglasses to cut the glare. He wasn't sure how long he'd been walking but didn't really care. He had nowhere to be.

He looked up and stopped abruptly. There they were again. Tally, Miss Mary, and Bobby, with the energetic puppy at their side. If he spun around now, before they saw him, they'd never even know he'd been here. He started to turn when he heard Bobby cry out. Squinting, he peered down the beach. Bobby was on the ground, and the women were hovering over him.

He sighed. Totally against his will, he jogged down the beach toward them. It's not like he could just ignore them now. Even he wasn't that cold.

"Hi. Everything okay?" He looked down and saw things were *not* okay.

"Bobby tripped and sliced his knee open on something. Maybe a sharp shell." Tally was drying the boy's tears.

Blood dripped down Bobby's leg, mixing with sand and seawater.

"I should call Eddie and see if he can come get us. I don't think Bobby can walk back like that."

"We're not far from the cafe. I'll carry him there." It's not like he could leave the boy here bleeding.

"Are you sure?" Tally looked up at him, concern plastered on her face.

"I'm sure." He reached a hand down to help her to her feet.

"I got tangled in Stormy's leash and *fell-ded* down."

"I can see that. How about I give you a piggyback ride? You think you could climb on my back?"

"I guess so. I'm gonna get blood on you, though."

"Not a problem." He knelt down by the boy, and Bobby climbed on his back. Sure enough, his shorts were soon covered with blood.

"I'll call Courtney and let her know what happened. She's working at the cafe." Tally slipped out her phone, made the call, then turned to Mary. "Mary, you come on with us. We'll give you and Stormy a ride back to the inn after we get Bobby taken care of."

"I could just walk back. I'll be okay."

"Oh, I know you would, but how about we get some tea after this long walk, and I'll run you back afterward?" Tally's words were casual, but the tone had an insistence to them. He wasn't sure what that was all about.

"Tea sounds nice."

The four of them plus the dog started down the beach toward the restaurant. The boy was surprisingly light and rested his head on AJ's shoulder. Before they got all the way to Magic Cafe, Courtney came running toward them.

"Bobby. Are you okay?" Panic covered her face, and she reached out to touch Bobby's leg.

"I'm okay. I cut my leg again."

"I see that." She looked closely at the wound then took in AJ's bloody clothes. "Sorry about this. Thank you so much for bringing him to me. I can take him now."

AJ eyed her and the distance left to the restaurant. "Nah, I've got him. You're okay up there, aren't you, buddy?"

"Mom, Mr. Hamilton's got me. I'm probably too big for you to carry me now that I'm six."

Courtney nodded anxiously. "Okay, well, thank you."

She hovered by his side as they walked the distance to the cafe, with Mary, Tally, and the dog trailing right behind them.

"Here, set him down on this chair." Tally motioned to a chair by the deck. "I'll go get the first aid kit."

He knelt down, and Bobby slipped off his back. "There you go, buddy."

"Thanks."

He looked at the blood on the boy's leg. "I'm going to go get water to wash that off."

"Thank you." Courtney knelt beside the boy,

her hands smoothing his hair and brushing sand off his leg, then moving back to pat his shoulder.

He took one more look at her motherly concern, a pang of remembrance stabbing through him. He turned away and closed his eyes for a moment. Just as quick as it had flashed through him, the fleeting memory was gone. He headed into the cafe.

Courtney tried to steady her hammering heart by taking a few deep breaths. When Tally had called and said Bobby had been hurt, she'd flown into an all-out panic, even though Tally had said it was just a cut on his leg.

She didn't think any mother could resist panic when they heard their child was hurt.

"You doing okay?" She reached up and pushed a lock of hair away from Bobby's face.

"Yeah. I'm okay. I can't believe I cut my leg again, though. Just like when Pops found me at that old gazebo and saved me. Now Mr. Hamilton saved me."

"He didn't actually *save* you."

"Well, he carried me back to Magic Cafe. Grams said I couldn't walk."

AJ returned with a pitcher of water. "Tereza got this for me." He knelt beside Bobby. "I'm going to dump this water on your leg, and we'll see what we have, okay?"

Bobby pulled back. "I don't know…" His eyes started to fill with tears.

"It will be fine, I promise. It might sting a little, but that's all." AJ's voice held a soothing, patient tone that took Courtney by surprise.

"Okay, I guess so." Bobby squeezed her hand and watched as AJ lifted the pitcher. He slowly poured the water on Bobby's leg and washed the sand away. A long cut wrapped its way down Bobby's leg.

"Got yourself a pretty good cut there." AJ peered at the wound.

"I'm always cutting my leg. I had to get stitches last time." The boy eyed him suspiciously. "I'm not going to have to get them this time, am I?"

"I'm not a doctor, but I don't think so," he assured the boy.

"Good, 'cause they aren't very fun."

"I think Mr. Hamilton is right. We'll get it cleaned up, and I think you'll be fine."

Tally hurried back with the first aid kit. "Here we go. Let me clean that with some antiseptic, and we'll wrap it up."

"I think you should let Mr. Hamilton do it. He's pretty good at this stuff."

"I…" AJ sat back on his heels.

"Oh, Bobby, Mr. Hamilton has done enough." Courtney put her hand on Bobby's knee.

"But he's good. See, he got the blood all gone, and it didn't hardly hurt."

"Here, hand me the kit. I'll do it." AJ reached for the kit. "This is going to sting, okay? But it gets the germs out."

Bobby nodded, bit his lip, and held onto her hand.

AJ carefully poured the liquid and used a gauze pad to finish cleaning the cut.

She watched while he gently took care of her son. Reassuring him, moving slowly and carefully, telling Bobby exactly what he was doing with each step. She hadn't expected this from a man whose eyes had flashed *escape, escape* when he'd found out she had a son. Maybe she'd judged him a bit too quickly. Maybe he'd just been surprised.

Maybe.

AJ wound a long wrap of gauze around the cut and taped it into place. "Good as new. Well, almost."

"You should be a doctor." Bobby looked at him solemnly. "You're good at this."

"Well, can't say I ever wanted to be one."

"What are you?"

"What am I?" AJ frowned in confusion.

"Yeah, you know. Like a fireman or astronaut or baseball player or something."

"None of those, I'm afraid. I'm just…"

Courtney looked at him. She didn't really know what he did.

"I'm just a businessman."

"Oh." Bobby looked disappointed. "Well, I guess someone has to be."

AJ laughed. "I guess they do."

"Well, I'm going to get Mary some tea then drive her and Stormy home. You all good here?" Tally picked up the first aid kit.

"Yes, we're fine. Thanks. I think Bobby deserves an ice cream after all of this." Courtney patted his leg.

"Mr. Hamilton, I'm hoping you'll come to dinner tonight at my house as a thank you." Tally stood looking down at AJ.

Courtney stared at Tally. *What was she doing?*

"We're having Courtney and Bobby over for dinner tonight. We'd love it if you'd come. About six?"

"I… uh…" AJ stood.

"That's a yes?" Tally smiled her welcoming smile

that no one could refuse. Courtney knew AJ didn't have a chance.

"Okay. Yes. That would be nice."

Courtney took a deep breath. So now she had to have dinner with this man again. Well, at least he'd get to see what a handful Bobby was. She was certain Bobby would be back to his normal whirlwind self by this evening.

And then AJ could go back to his normal reaction to Bobby. Scared.

CHAPTER 8

Tally slipped a homemade peach pie into the oven. She was enjoying cooking again. Before Eddie came back, she mostly just grabbed something at Magic Cafe.

Eddie walked into the kitchen, carrying a package of fresh fish. "I got the grouper like you wanted."

"Thanks. I think grilled grouper, a salad, rolls, and pie will be a good meal, don't you? I got the pie from The Sweet Shoppe. Julie made fresh peach pie today. I just have to finish baking it."

"Sounds great. This fella is lucky he picked today to help with Bobby." Eddie grinned mischievously. "It was nice of you to ask him to dinner to thank him."

Tally smiled. "Well, that's not the only reason. I

asked him because I've seen the way Courtney looks at him."

Eddie laughed. "Ah, you're a clever woman. Like that about you." He leaned down and kissed her.

She still couldn't get used to the fact Eddie was here every day. Smiling at her. Kissing her. Laughing with her. Tally wondered if she'd ever get used to it. She hoped not. She hoped that each day would stay as special as it seemed now.

Eddie put the fish in the fridge. "You're always trying to give everyone their happy ending, huh?"

"Oh, I don't know about a happy ending, but I think it's high time she dated some men now that Kurt is out of her life."

"He darn well better be out of her life if he knows what's good for him. I'm annoyed his lawyer got him out on bail, but hopefully, when the case goes to court, he'll get the book thrown at him. He still has the restraining order against him, and I'm sure his lawyer made it perfectly clear that he was to stay far, far away from Courtney and Bobby. I don't think Kurt is dumb enough to make things worse for his trial."

"I hope not." Tally walked over to where she had everything out to make a nice fresh garden salad.

Eddie started to walk out of the kitchen and turned back. "Tally?"

"Hm?" She looked up from where she was chopping up a carrot.

"I love you." He winked at her and walked out of the room.

She started humming while she finished preparing the meal.

Courtney stood in front of her closet, once again trying to figure out what to wear. She didn't know why AJ threw her off balance, but he did. Okay, he was exceptionally good-looking, she'd give him that, but she refused to fall under the spell of his dazzle-the-ladies smile. Refused.

It was probably just that she hadn't dated so long before going out with him. Not that tonight was a date…

She finally chose a simple sundress and pink sandals. After dressing, she walked out of her bedroom. "Bobby, you about ready? We'll drive. I'm not sure you can walk tonight."

"Momma, I'm fine. Let's walk. I like walking to Grams and Pops' house."

Bobby had changed into clean shorts and a

bright t-shirt Tally had given him that said "Make a Wish at Lighthouse Point." He did look like he felt fine. Kids sure bounce back quickly. "Okay, we'll walk."

They went outside, and she closed and locked the door. Bobby slipped his hand in hers, and they headed for Tally's. Bobby chattered the whole way, of course.

"And even though I got hurt walking Stormy, it doesn't mean I can't have a dog of my own, right?"

"Bobby, we've talked about it. Now is not the time to get a dog."

"Aw, Mom."

"Look, there's Pops." She changed the subject and waved to Eddie. Bobby slipped his hand from hers and ran up to him.

"Look. I got hurt again. Just like when you saved me. Only this time Mr. Hamilton saved me."

"I heard about that." Eddie swung the boy up in his arms. "Come on, champ. Let's go out back and start the grill."

She watched as Eddie and Bobby went around to the back of the cottage then turned to head up onto the porch.

"Hi, Courtney."

She spun around at the sound of her name. AJ stood just a few steps away, dressed in nice shorts and a collared short-sleeve shirt. The sun glistened off his hair, his face glowed a ruddy tan from his days on the island, and his brown eyes twinkled as he smiled at her. He held a bouquet of flowers in his hand.

"Hi." Honestly, he was so good-looking, it almost took her breath away, which was ridiculous, because she was immune to that kind of thing. Especially from someone afraid of kids. She cleared her throat, rapped once, and opened the door. "Tally, we're here."

"Back in the kitchen."

AJ held the door open for her as she slipped inside. She brushed past him, a bit too close for comfort. They headed to the kitchen.

"These are for you." He handed the flowers to Tally.

"Well, thank you. You didn't need to do that, though. This is a thank you dinner for your help with Bobby."

"I appreciate the invite. Can't tell you the last time I had a home-cooked meal."

"Courtney, why don't you two grab some drinks and head out back while Eddie grills."

"I should stay in and help you."

"No, I'm almost finished. I'll join you in a few minutes. Go on out."

They grabbed a couple of beers and headed outside. Eddie tossed a baseball to Bobby while he let the coals heat up.

"Hi, Momma. Hi, Mr. Hamilton." Bobby waved then smacked a fist into his glove and waited for Eddie to pitch the ball back to him.

"Eddie is wonderful with him." Courtney took a seat on the glider but then instantly regretted the decision.

AJ walked over and plopped down beside her, stretching out his long, tanned legs, just inches from her. "So, if you don't mind me asking…"

She eyed him, wondering what he wanted to know. "No, go ahead and ask."

"Bobby calls them Grams and Pops, but you call them by their first names."

"I know. It's just… that's how I got to know them first. Before I knew they were my grandparents."

"You didn't know they were your grandparents?"

"It's a long story, but we just found out this year. My father was Tally's son. He's dead. He was lost at sea. My mother…" Courtney looked away for a moment and took a sip of her drink. "She died in childbirth when she had me."

"I'm so sorry."

"So, I never knew my parents. But we pieced it

together after Bobby and I got to town. I'm so lucky to have found them."

"They seem pretty happy to have found you two, also."

AJ set the glider in slow motion, and they sat and watched Bobby play catch. Now that AJ had asked her, she wondered if she should be calling Tally and Eddie something else? Was it hurting their feelings that she called them by their first names?

Like she needed one more thing to overthink in her life. She mentally shook her head at herself if that were even possible.

Tally came out the door with a pitcher of lemonade. "Bobby, you want some?"

Bobby came racing up. "Yes, ma'am." He took the glass from Tally.

Tally poured Eddie a glass, walked over, and gave it to him. Eddie smiled at her, and she lit up. Courtney loved watching the two of them together. So happy after so many years apart.

"Pops said I get to flip the fish over. I'm big enough for that."

"Just be careful. The grill is hot."

"I know, Momma. I'm a big kid now, remember?"

She smiled at him. "I remember."

"How's that leg doing?" AJ asked.

"It's okay. But Momma is treating me like a baby. She thought we couldn't even walk over here." Bobby let out a long sigh then turned and skipped back over to where Eddie was putting the fish on the grill.

"Why walk when you can skip?" AJ grinned in amusement.

"He is constant energy. Always."

They sat in companionable silence while Eddie grilled the fish. He took it up, and they all headed inside and sat around the big kitchen table.

"I thought I only liked fish that was in sticks, but then I had Pops' fish. It's the best ever." Bobby swung his legs as he sat on his chair.

They talked and laughed, and Courtney enjoyed every single minute of it. She'd never had a family dinner before finding Tally and Eddie. The simple joy of just eating and laughing almost choked her up. She sat back and listened to the talk and watched as Bobby cleaned his plate and finished off a piece of the delicious peach pie.

Eddie pushed his plate away. "That was a great meal."

"Thank you." Tally glowed at the praise.

"It was." Courtney wished she could find time to make meals like this for Bobby every night.

"Well, the pie was from Julie."

"The whole meal was wonderful. Thank you for inviting me." AJ scooted his chair back and relaxed.

"So, I'm trying to talk Tally into going away for a few days. The two of us." Eddie took Tally's hand and threw a look Courtney's way, asking for help.

"That's a great idea." Courtney leaned forward.

"I couldn't leave Magic Cafe."

"Of course you could. You've taught me a lot. And Tereza will help. We'll be fine."

"See?" Eddie's eyes sparkled as he looked at Tally.

"I don't know…"

"Say 'yes.' You two never even had a honeymoon."

"Didn't need one. I have everything I need right here." Tally looked at Eddie and sighed. "But if you really want to go away, we could. Just a few days though."

Courtney clapped her hands. "This is great. You'll have fun. It will be nice to get away from it all for a few days. You should go soon."

"I'll plan everything. You don't have to do a thing. I promise." Eddie squeezed Tally's hand then stood. "Come on, Bobby. Let's clear the table. What do you say? Then we'll go in the front room, and I'll read some more of that chapter book we've been reading."

"Eddie, you and Bobby go read. I'll help with the dishes." AJ stood and gathered some plates.

"You don't have to do that. You're our guest," Tally protested.

"I don't mind. Not at all."

Courtney watched as AJ balanced some plates and headed over to the sink. She jumped up to help and stood beside him at the counter, near enough to touch him and feeling strangely jumpy at the closeness. He smelled of a faint, clean, woodsy scent. He turned and smiled at her, and she almost dropped the dish she was holding.

From the corner of her eye, she saw Tally smile and shake her head. Her grandmother didn't miss much of anything, and she was beginning to believe this dinner was less of a thank you and more of a let's fix Courtney up.

CHAPTER 9

A J couldn't believe what a wonderful time he was having. Just a simple family meal. But they never made him feel like he wasn't welcome or like an outsider. He felt more at home at their kitchen table than he did at his own father's house.

He helped Tally and Courtney with the dishes, something he'd never done before past just rinsing a few of his own dishes and throwing them in the dishwasher. And most of the time, he ate takeout or leftovers from some meal he'd had at a restaurant. His cupboards were usually fairly bare except for the ever-present coffee.

They finished doing the dishes, and he followed Tally and Courtney into the front room. He paused in the doorway. Bobby was sound asleep on the couch, curled up against Eddie.

"You know, why don't you just leave Bobby here for the night? We'll just carry him up to bed. There's no reason to wake him up to take him home." Tally walked over and draped an afghan over Bobby.

Courtney bit her lip. "I guess so."

"I'll bring him to Magic Cafe with me tomorrow. You're working the early shift, right? How does that sound?" Tally turned to Courtney.

"Okay. That's probably better than waking him up to walk back to our apartment." Courtney leaned down and kissed Bobby, smoothing his hair from his face. She paused and stared at him for a moment, her expression filled with love. "I should probably go now. I do have an early morning."

The look hit him hard. That look of a mother for their child. His mother had probably looked at him like that, too, but he couldn't remember. He had so few memories of her, and his father certainly hadn't filled in any of the blanks.

He pulled himself back to the present. "I should go, too. Thanks again for the invite. I had a wonderful time."

"You're more than welcome. We'll do it again." Tally walked them to the door.

He and Courtney walked outside into the balmy night air. The sky had darkened, and stars broke through in brilliant speckles of light.

She turned to him. "Well, I guess this is good night. I really do appreciate your help with Bobby today."

"Can I walk you home?"

"You don't have to do that."

"But I'd like to." He didn't like the idea of her walking herself home alone, even if the island was one of the safest places he'd been to.

"Okay."

It wasn't much of an enthusiastic agreement, but he'd take it. She turned to head down the sidewalk.

He walked beside her in the silence. One lone car slowly passed them, then darkness surrounded them again. Music softly drifted out from a house as they walked by. A dog barked in the distance.

He wanted to take her hand, connect with her, but wavered in his decision until he decided he better not. And why he wanted to walk hand in hand was beyond him. It wasn't something he normally did. Like ever.

They turned into a lot surrounded by separate bungalows, each painted a different, bright color. She stopped in front of a teal bungalow with pretty flowers planted outside. "This is me."

"These are nice."

"They are. We just moved here a few days ago."

She put her key in the lock then paused after she turned it. "Um… would you like to come in for a few minutes?"

"I would." He wasn't really ready for the night to end.

She stepped inside and flipped on the lights. A few lamps illuminated the sparsely furnished apartment. She picked up a truck and a baseball bat on the floor and set them in the corner by a stack of boxes. "Sorry, it's kind of a mess. I haven't had much time to unpack yet."

"That's okay."

"I—" She stood in the middle of the room, looking undecided. "Would you like a drink? I have a couple of beers in the fridge or an open bottle of wine. That's all I have to offer."

"A beer would be great."

She went to the fridge and grabbed two beers. "We could sit outside on the bench. It's a nice night out."

They headed back out and sat on a white wooden bench outside her door. She kicked off her sandals. Her thigh brushed against his as she stretched out her long, slender legs. Her toenails were painted a bright pink. He deliberately ignored her leg resting against his and took a long swallow of his beer. Then another. Why did this woman get to him? He barely knew her.

"I love these warm summer nights on the island. Though, it seems like summer goes through October or November down here, not that I'm complaining." She picked at the corner of the label on her beer bottle.

"I'm all for non-winter weather. Well, except for skiing. I do love to ski."

"I've never been." She turned and looked at him with her luminous blue eyes.

He could get lost in those eyes. Which was ridiculous because, as he just told himself, he hardly knew her. And she was nothing like the women he dated. She wasn't his type. Not at all. She probably would hate to go clubbing. He knew she'd dislike the friends he hung out with. Not that they were really *friends*, per se. They were just the crowd he ran with.

But none of that mattered right now, because he was right where he wanted to be. Except that bothered him somewhat... How could he be content with a night that consisted of a family dinner, a leisurely stroll, and just sitting on a bench in the moonlight?

Yet, he *was* strangely content tonight. A feeling

that he hadn't felt in... well, he couldn't remember ever feeling like this.

What had he been talking about? He had no clue. His mind just bopped around from thought to thought.

"Do you go skiing often?" She sent him a look that made him think her question was more than just small talk. Like she was really interested in his answer. Like... like she really wanted to get to know him better.

Ah, he'd been talking about skiing. "I try and go a couple times a season."

"What's it like to go soaring down the slopes? I always imagined it would feel like you were flying, the wind brushing your cheeks, that it would feel so... free."

For someone who'd never been, she'd described it perfectly. "That's it exactly. You should try it sometime."

"Well, I pretty much have my hands full right now. I will someday though."

He couldn't miss the wistful look in her eyes. He wished he could whisk her off to the slopes right now, teach her to ski, and let her swoosh down the slopes with him. He could just picture her face, her eyes wide with amazement and awe. And he'd love to be the one to put that look on her face and share the experience with her.

Whoa.

He needed to slow down and stop the crazy thoughts.

But he couldn't help himself.

"So…" He paused and took a breath. "Do you think we could try going out again?"

She looked at him directly. "I thought Bobby scared you off."

"He…" He paused and shrugged. "I *was* surprised, I admit. I'm not used to children. But Bobby seems like a good kid."

"He is. He's my whole world." She took a sip of her beer. "So, I think it would be better if we just… left it like it is. I'll see you if you come by Magic Cafe—you don't need to stay away because of me. But I think maybe I'm not ready to date."

Disappointment swelled through him, which annoyed him no end. Since when did he care if a woman turned him down? Not that many did…

"If you're sure that's what you want."

"I'm sure."

But her voice didn't sound like she was exactly sure. He'd drop by Magic Cafe and keep trying to ask her out. He wanted to spend more time with her. He wanted more simple, easy-going outings with her. He wanted… he raked his hand through his hair.

The sad fact was he didn't know what he wanted anymore.

Courtney leaned against the doorframe and watched as AJ headed back to his rental. She was certain she made the right decision to not go out with him again.

Fairly certain. *Kind of* certain.

It did seem he'd warmed up to Bobby a little bit. She didn't need another complication in her life. Her life was perfect now with Bobby thriving and Tally and Eddie in their lives. She had a job that supported her and Bobby. Bobby had a family that loved him, something she'd never had growing up.

Why would she go and complicate all that by dating some guy who was here for a month or less? A rich guy that ran in different circles than she. Circles she'd never run in or ever want to run in for that matter.

A bit of a shiver trilled through her, and she glanced around the empty courtyard between the cottages. She rubbed her hands on her arms, feeling the instant goosebumps. A slow scan of the area revealed nothing out of sorts.

She turned around and went inside, carefully locking the door behind her. With brisk steps, she walked to each window and made sure the blinds were firmly closed.

It must just be that the place was new to her. She didn't usually get spooked over nothing. She swept a look around the front room. Nothing seemed out of place. It was deathly quiet without Bobby, though. She didn't think she liked this deal of him staying over at Tally and Eddie's. She wasn't used to being alone. That was all it was.

She reached over to turn out the lamp but then just turned it lower so it cast a faint illumination in the front room. With one last look around, she headed back to her bedroom.

Feeling foolish, she locked the door to her bedroom behind her.

CHAPTER 10

AJ already regretted going into Sarasota to the new club with Camille and Delbert tonight. The whole scene didn't even appeal to him anymore. Delbert chatted with other movers and shakers in the town. Camille was… being Camille. Making fun of some of the women's outfits and hairdos. Complaining about the food. He glanced at his watch for like the tenth time in an hour. The evening dragged on and on. He smiled and tried to make small talk with Camille, unsure when he could make his excuses and beg off.

He leaned back in his chair and watched some fairly drunk guy lurch across the floor to the bar. The man stopped by a woman sitting alone and said something to her, flinging his arm while he spoke and sloshing his drink. She shook her head no. The guy leaned in toward her, and she pushed him back.

AJ sprung to his feet and crossed the distance to the bar. "Is he bothering you, ma'am?"

She looked at him gratefully and nodded. "I just asked him to go away."

"But, little lady, you didn't mean it. Let me get ya a drink." The man slurred his words.

"No, thank you." The woman scooted to the far edge of her stool.

"How about you just move on?" AJ stepped closer to the man.

"Or what?"

"I just think it would be best if you moved on down the bar."

"Why, so you can get this sweet thing a drink?"

"First off, quit calling the lady names. Second off, you've had too much to drink."

"Mind your own business." The man stumbled to the side and swung a punch toward AJ. AJ ducked to the side, and the man fell forward and caught the lady's arm with his fist. She cried out.

AJ slipped in between the man and the woman. "It's time for you to leave." His voice was low and threatening.

"I don't think so." The man raised his fist, and

AJ easily caught his wrist and held firmly, preventing another punch.

"You need some help, Jonny?" Two burly men walked up. There was no other way to describe them. Big. Tall. And they each had a hundred pounds on him. At least.

"Yeah, this joker won't let me talk to the lady."

"Is that so?"

One of the big guys threw a punch and caught AJ under the jaw. The lady fled from her stool to safety. AJ shook his head, trying to clear his vision. The three men lunged toward him, though he managed to right himself and step back.

From behind the men, he saw a group of police rush into the club.

Great. *Now* they show up.

Cameras flashed. The manager hurried over. "Take them all."

"Wait." AJ stood frozen.

"All of them. We won't have this nonsense in my club."

"I was just…"

"Save it." A policeman reached out to cuff him.

Delbert hurried up to them. "Really? The police? You can't stay out of trouble for one night?" His cousin looked at him in dismay. "When are you ever going to grow up?"

Hot anger flashed through him. Delbert. His cousin, too. He was just like the rest of his family who always thought the worst of him.

"Officer." The lady slipped up by his side and placed a hand on the policeman's arm. "This man was just trying to help me. That man—" She pointed to the drunken man. "He hit me. This man was just *protecting* me."

The policeman looked at the manager, who frowned then nodded. The policeman put away the cuffs.

The lady handed AJ a napkin. "Here, you have a bit of blood by your lip."

He took the napkin and dapped at his face.

The lady then whirled around and faced off with Delbert. "This man—" She turned to AJ. "What's your name?"

"AJ."

"AJ saved me from a man who was getting rough. The man punched me, and AJ stepped in."

Delbert turned to him. "I'm sorry... I just assumed..."

"Right. I know. My family always assumes the worst of me." He turned away from his cousin.

The lady stood by his side while the police led the other three men out of the club. She turned to him. "Really, thank you so much for your help."

"Are you okay? You took a pretty good punch there."

She rubbed her arm. "I'll be okay."

"If you're sure you're okay now, I'll be leaving."

"I'm fine. I can't thank you enough for your help. My name is Lynn. Lynn Miller."

"Nice to meet you, Miss Miller. I hope the rest of your evening is uneventful."

"AJ, wait." Delbert reached out his hand and caught his arm.

AJ shook his head and shrugged off Delbert's hand. He turned on his heels and, without a word to Delbert or Camille, strode out of the club and into the fresh night air. Out of the noise. Away from the accusations.

He climbed into his car, rolled down the windows, and let the warm night air sweep over him. He headed back to Belle Island. The island called to him with its sweet siren lure of tranquility and peace.

AJ slept fitfully and finally dozed off in the early morning hours. He awoke with the sun streaming in his windows, much later than he usually slept.

After a quick shower, he wandered down to the kitchen in search of coffee.

His grandmother stopped him as he entered the room. "Ashton, your father has already called this morning. He's not pleased."

He let out a long, tired sigh. "What is it this time?"

Granice held out the paper, folded precisely so a photo of him, blood on his face, stared back at him.

"Oh, that." He couldn't believe that skirmish hit the gossip page.

"He asked you to stay out of trouble."

"I have. I—" He thrust the paper back to her. "Everyone in this family always thinks the worst of me. That photo—it's not what it looks like." He stalked to the kitchen and poured a cup of coffee.

"Ashton, wait." Granice tried to stop him, but he bounded up the stairs to his room to drink his coffee in peace. He didn't even try to explain to her. He was done explaining to his family.

He walked out onto the balcony and sat on a stool by the railing. He refused to admit it stung that Granice had jumped to the conclusion he'd gotten into some kind of brawl. Which, if a person wanted to get technical, he had. But it had only been to step in and help that woman. What was her name? Lynn something. There was no way he could have just ignored that man pestering her. The man had punched her, for Pete's sake. Who could ignore that?

He watched as a sleek boat glided along the shore with a swell of wake following along behind it. A family of four had placed a pop-up canopy near the shoreline, and two school-aged boys frolicked in the waves, their dad standing at the edge of the water, watching them, and their mother settled in a chair, reading. Just a normal family.

Not that he had any clue what that would be like.

CHAPTER 11

Courtney, Tereza, and Tally took a quick break after the breakfast rush. Tally poured them each a tall glass of iced tea. Courtney sank gratefully into a chair, glad to have a few moments to rest her feet. Tereza and Tally grabbed seats across from her.

"It's going to be a hot one today. Temperature is already at ninety." Tereza fanned herself with a page of the newspaper. They always had papers scattered around for their customers to read with their breakfasts.

"I heard a storm is coming in tomorrow. That should break this heat streak." Courtney took a sip of her tea then pressed the cool glass against her forehead.

Tereza looked at the paper she held in her hand

and unfolded it. "Hey, look at this. It's AJ." She handed the paper to Courtney.

She opened the paper and stared at the photo of AJ. He had a bit of blood on his face, his hair was rumpled, and police stood at his side, handcuffs in hand. She scanned the story. "Looks like he was in some kind of bar fight at a new club in Sarasota."

Tally reached for the paper. "Hmm. Not many details. Just says he was involved in a scuffle at the club. Wonder what happened?"

"Well, I guess I'm even gladder I didn't agree to go out with him again if he's the type who gets into fights in bars."

"He asked you out again?" Tereza pushed damp wisps of her hair away from her face.

"He did... but I said I didn't think it would be a good thing."

"Because?" Tereza scowled at her with an accusing look.

"Because Bobby scares him. Because... well, look. He's fighting in a bar."

"Don't you think you should hear his side of the story for this photo?" Tally set the paper on the table. "And some people aren't used to kids. Haven't been around them. Doesn't mean they can't figure it out."

"Tally, are you still trying to fix us up?" She

dipped her chin and sent Tally an I-know-what-you're-up-to look.

"I'm not trying to do anything. I just like the man. I think you could give him a chance."

Eddie hurried up to the table, a huge smile on his face. "Well, I did it."

"Did what?" Tally looked up at him, a spontaneous smile on her face.

Eddie swooped into a chair beside Tally and dropped his arm around her shoulder. "I made all the plans for our getaway. We're going this next weekend."

"We can't." Tally's eyes grew wide.

"Yes, you can," Courtney and Tereza said in unison.

"But the restaurant and Bobby and... well, everything."

"We've got Magic Cafe covered, don't we, Tereza?"

"We sure do. We'll make sure everything goes smoothly." Tereza raised her glass, and Courtney clinked hers against it.

"See, everything is set." Eddie beamed.

Tally's eyes were filled with doubt. "But—"

"Really, Tally, I promise everything will be fine. Go on a trip with Eddie. Just go and relax and have fun." She reached over and took Tally's hand.

She just hoped she was right and she could keep everything running smoothly while Tally and Eddie got a much-deserved vacation.

AJ walked to Magic Cafe after the lunch crowd should have abated, hoping to see Courtney during the afternoon lull. He wasn't hungry but thought some sweet tea would be good. He hadn't realized how much it had warmed up, and how little breeze there was today. His shirt clung to his back. AJ stopped at the spigot by the stairs and splashed water on his face, the cool water refreshing on his hot skin.

He climbed up the steps from the beach, and Tally gave him the genuine welcoming smile he was beginning to get used to and like. "AJ, good to see you. Let me get you a table."

She led him to a table directly under a ceiling fan. "This should help keep you cool. It's a scorcher today."

"That it is." He sank into the chair and relished the breeze from the fan.

"Can I bring you something to drink?"

"Sweet tea, thanks."

"I'll send it over with Courtney. It's about time for her break. I'll get her to join you."

He was liking Tally more and more. Here she was doing half his work for him. He smiled as she walked away. She stopped and talked to Courtney. It looked like Courtney argued with her then went over to the bar.

Soon Courtney arrived with a tea and two large glasses of water. "You look hot." She handed him the tea and one water.

"Join me?"

She nodded, sat across from him, and shoved some locks of hair away from her face. Her face blushed pink from the heat. "Tally practically ordered me to take a break. I can only sit a few minutes, though."

He took a long swallow of the ice water. "That is just what I needed."

"You walked over?"

"I did. Didn't realize there wasn't much breeze today."

She pressed her glass against her face, and condensation ran down her cheek then down her neck. He swallowed and turned his stare from trailing after the drops of water.

Unaware of his gaze, Courtney leaned back in

her chair. "So… I saw your photo in the paper today."

Here it comes. The chastising, the accusations.

"What happened? You okay?"

He sat there, a bit stunned someone was actually *asking* him what happened instead of accusing him of something. "Well, there was this lady, and this drunk was getting pushy with her. He wasn't taking no, and I kind of stepped in."

"Like a knight in shining armor kind of rescue?" She rewarded him with a grin of amusement, her eyes lighting up mischievously.

"Something like that." He relaxed in his seat, basking in her teasing and her acceptance of his explanation. "Bit of a mix-up with the cops until the lady straightened things out."

"You've got a bruise on your face."

He reached up and touched his cheek. "Yeah, one of the guys clipped me good."

"I'm glad you weren't hurt worse, and I'm glad you were there to help the woman. It was rather… gallant of you."

Gallant. She thought he was gallant. He could feel a goofy grin spread across his face. He figured he'd press his advantage. "So, does that mean you'll go out with me again?" He sent her his best boyish charm smile.

She sat for a moment then nodded. "I guess I can't very well refuse to go out with a hero, now can I?"

"It's probably against the official hero protocol."

She smothered a smile. "I'm not well versed in hero rules of dating, but I guess I can learn them."

"Now would be as good a time as any."

"I'm off tonight if that's not too late of notice."

He was liking how this day was turning out. "Not at all. I could pick you up about six?"

"That sounds great." She took one last sip of her water and stood. "I'd better get back to work. I'll see you tonight."

"I'll see you then." He watched her walk away, grinning at his good luck.

CHAPTER 12

E ddie offered to watch Bobby while Courtney went on her date. He seemed glad she was going. She couldn't get used to having family here. Family who offered to help all the time, family who watched Bobby for her. She'd gotten so lucky and never stopped appreciating that Eddie and Tally were in her and Bobby's lives now.

She pulled on her one other sundress she owned. She'd now worn every outfit she had that was "date worthy." She took one last look in the mirror to check if she'd wiped away the last vestige of damage from the oppressive heat today and went out into the main room, picking up stray toys and punching some pillows into submission on the couch.

Promptly at six, she heard a knock at the door.

With a quick tuck of a flyaway wisp of hair, she hurried to the door.

AJ stood with a bouquet of flowers and smile. "These are for you."

"Thank you." She reached for them then stepped aside. "Come in. I'll put them in some water."

He slipped past her, and she closed the door behind him. She walked to the kitchen, and he followed her. His fresh, woodsy scent she'd come to recognize floated around her like a warm, welcoming quilt.

AJ watched while she set the flowers on the counter and opened one cabinet then the next one. Her face was flushed again, either from the heat or nerves, he wasn't sure. Whatever the cause, she looked lovely. A wave of attraction plunged through him.

"I can't seem to find a vase." Her tone said she was oblivious to the tension he was feeling.

She opened another cabinet and started to reach inside.

"You look very pretty tonight."

She paused in her search and turned to him.

In an instant, he was at her side and thrust his

hand out to catch the vase teetering on the edge of the shelf before it crashed to the floor.

She screamed and shrank away from him, her eyes wide with pure fright.

"I… uh… the vase." He held it precariously in one hand and took a step toward her.

She backed away, both hands held up in front of her. Fear was clearly etched across her face. Her eyes burned with a dazed confusion.

He frowned and stepped back, carefully setting the vase on the counter. "The vase was falling."

"I—" Her hand went up to her neck.

"Are you okay?" He narrowed his eyes, concerned and searching for what he'd done to cause her reaction. She must have been startled from the falling vase? Though, she didn't seem the skittish type.

She looked to the left and the right of him as if searching for an escape. He stepped back again. "Courtney? Are you okay?"

She crept back another step, tears hovering in the corner of her eyes. She shook her head.

He reached out a hand, but she backed away again even further. "Okay, it's okay. I'm sorry I scared you." He lowered his voice and murmured the words. "It's okay."

She leaned against the counter, clutching the edge with one hand, her knuckles white.

"Court…" He didn't know what was wrong, but something was. Something was very wrong. He took another step back, giving her space.

She swiped at a tear trailing down her cheek.

"Tell me. What's wrong?"

She shuddered and sucked in a long breath. As she released it, her hand dropped from the counter. "I… I'm sorry. I overreacted."

"I didn't mean to frighten you."

"I… I thought… I thought you…" She shuddered again. "I thought you were going to hit me."

He stood in stunned silence. Her pale face emphasized the truth of her words. She'd thought he was going to *hit* her.

Hit. Her.

"I… I can't imagine what I ever did…" Why would she think that of him? He'd thought she was different, but she was *just* like all the others, thinking the worst of him because he'd had his photo in the paper. A stupid scuffle in a bar. He'd explained it. He'd thought she understood.

So much for her words about him being a hero or gallant.

She was *afraid* of him.

"Don't worry. I'm leaving." He backed away, holding out his hands, palms up. He whirled around, headed to the door, and jerked it open. "I wasn't going to hit you. I'm sorry you think I'm the type of man… I can't believe you think that of me. Goodbye, Courtney."

He strode out the door and closed it firmly, just barely resisting the urge to slam it behind him.

"AJ, wait." But her words were barely above a whisper. She took a step forward, to go after him, but her legs gave out. Sinking to the floor, she stared at her trembling hands. She clasped them together.

Her heart pounded in her chest, and she gulped the air, trying to suck in enough oxygen to catch her breath. Hot tears trailed down her cheeks, and she didn't even try to stop them.

She'd been so certain he was getting ready to hit her when she saw his hand rise up by her face. It was like history repeating itself. She'd steeled herself for the coming pain of the blow.

But it hadn't come.

AJ hadn't been reaching to hit her, he was rescuing her vase.

She reached her hand up to her cheek like she had so many times before, but this time there was no sting, no pain, no blood. No need for makeup tomorrow to cover an angry bruise.

This.

This is what her life had become. Kurt had ruined her. Ruined her chances to have a normal relationship with another man.

She just couldn't bring herself to trust.

She let herself cry ugly sobs, her whole body spasming with each gulp of air until she had no more energy left. Then, slowly, she got on her knees and pulled herself up with the counter's edge.

She knew what she needed, what she wanted. She reached for her cell phone and called Tally.

CHAPTER 13

Tally tapped off her cell phone and turned to Tereza, worry rushing through her. "I have to go. It's Courtney. You got everything here?" She glanced around Magic Cafe and the busy crowd. "I hate to leave, but…"

"Not a problem. I've got this. Go see what Courtney needs." Tereza grabbed a tray of food, balanced it on her hip, and grabbed a pitcher of water.

"Thanks." Tally hurried out, wishing she had her car, but she'd walked to work tonight. She walked at a brisk pace to Courtney's bungalow.

She knocked on the door. "Courtney?"

The door swung open after a few moments. Courtney stood in the doorway, her face pale and eyes red from crying. Tally opened her arms, and

Courtney collapsed into them. Tally maneuvered them both inside and closed the door. "There, there." She patted Courtney's shoulder.

Courtney finally pulled back and swiped her palms across her cheeks, streaking the stream of tears.

"Now, can you tell me what happened?" Tally led her over to the couch, grabbed a tissue, and pressed it into Courtney's hands.

Courtney dried her tears, blew her nose, and took a deep breath. "I… I thought that… I thought AJ was going to hit me."

"What?" Tally sank onto the couch next to Courtney and frowned. "He doesn't seem like—"

"He's not." Courtney leaned back on the couch. "He was just reaching to catch a vase that was falling from the cabinet. But when I saw his hand coming toward my face… well, I freaked out."

"That's understandable." Tally patted her leg, trying to reassure her.

"But… I just lost it. I couldn't quite wrap my head around the fact he wasn't… hitting me."

Tally leaned forward and hugged her granddaughter. "I think that's a normal reaction after all you went through with Kurt."

Courtney nodded. "But I think I hurt AJ's

feelings. I told him I thought he was going to hit me."

"But you explained why you thought that, right?"

"No… I didn't know how to, and he didn't give me any time. He stormed out of here, not that I blame him." Courtney leaned over and grabbed another tissue from the box beside the couch. "I really messed this up."

"I think you should tell him what happened. Tell him about Kurt. He'll understand." Tally's heart broke for all her granddaughter had endured. The abuse, the fear. She was so thankful all of that was behind her now. But she could understand why Courtney reacted how she did when AJ reached past her face.

"I don't know how to tell him. I feel so ridiculous for not leaving Kurt sooner. I was so young and naive. For so long I believed him when he said I did things that made him hit me." Courtney shook her head. "I was so… foolish."

"It is not your fault." Tally was stunned by her granddaughter's words. She hadn't realized Courtney blamed herself. "You did leave. You got Bobby to safety."

"But I let it go on so long. Believed Kurt. If I tell AJ everything, he'll know how foolish I was."

"None of this is your fault. None. It took strength to leave him. To believe in yourself instead of Kurt's words. That's what abusers do. They convince you that somehow if you'd just be better, just act more how they wanted you to, then they wouldn't get mad and hit you." She took Courtney's hand. "But you are one of the strongest women I know. Look how far you've come. Look what a fabulous mother you are. You should feel proud of yourself for escaping your background and making such a good life for you and Bobby."

Her granddaughter's brows knitted together in doubt. Tears filled her eyes again like an unrelenting storm.

Tally reached over and touched Courtney's cheek. "I'd give anything to take away what happened to you. If things could have been different for you and Bobby. I just thank God every single day that you and Bobby were brought into my life. That I found you."

Courtney leaned against her and started crying softly. "I'm so glad we found you, too."

Tally just held her and let her cry. Tally's heart clenched, and she physically ached to see her granddaughter in such distress.

Courtney finally quieted and pushed herself up, swiping away the last of her tears. "Thank you for being here for me." She fingered the rose gold pocket watch hanging from the chain around her neck as if gathering comfort from the mother she never knew.

"Always." Tally smiled at her granddaughter's caress of the heirloom. "I think you should tell AJ what happened though. Tell him everything. He'll understand."

Courtney sighed and pushed her hair away from her face. "You're probably right."

"It will do you good to tell him. It's not a terrible secret you need to keep. Kurt is a horrible human being, but he is your past. Maybe AJ can help you move on." Tally paused and looked directly into Courtney's eyes. "I do think AJ is a good man. I like him."

"I guess I'll tell him. *If* I ever even see him again. He was pretty upset with me."

"I think tonight is the perfect time to tell him." She eyed Courtney.

"I don't know."

"I do. I think you should call him, meet him, tell him."

Courtney's lips curved into the hint of a smile. "Man, you're a tough one, aren't you?"

"I am. Especially with those I love."

~

Courtney called AJ, but he didn't pick up. Not that she really expected him to. She left him a brief message saying she wanted to talk to him. Then she texted him for good measure, telling him she was sorry and needed to talk.

Still no answer.

Tally's phone rang, and she quickly answered it. "Hey, Susan, I'm over at Courtney's new place, can I call you back? No, she's fine. She's just trying to find AJ Hamilton."

Tally looked over and tilted her head. "Really? Well, that helps. Thanks, Susan." She tapped off the phone and stood. "Let's go."

"Where are we going? I'm a mess."

"Go wash your face then. We're headed to The Lucky Duck. Susan's son, Jamie, saw AJ there. He's sitting at the bar drinking a beer. "

Courtney didn't even question how all this happened and suddenly AJ was found. Susan, Julie, and Tally always seemed to know everything about everyone on the island.

"Give me just a minute." Courtney hurried to her bathroom, splashed water on her face, and threw on just a hint of makeup. She quickly returned to the front room. "I'm ready."

"Good, let's go." Tally opened the door, and they walked out into the salty night air.

They quickly made their way to The Lucky Duck. Tally stood inside the door with her and nodded toward the bar where AJ sat nursing a beer. "Go. Talk to him. I'll talk to you later. Call me if you need me." With that, Tally turned around and walked out of the tavern, leaving Courtney alone to slay her dragon.

She dragged in a breath of fortifying air, walked over, and slipped onto the barstool next to AJ. "Hi."

AJ glanced up at Courtney then went back to methodically eating the nuts out of a small bowl in front of him.

"I tried calling. I texted."

"Yep." He tilted back his head and took a long swallow of his beer, still not looking at her.

"AJ, can I please talk to you? I know you're mad, but please let me explain."

"Not much to explain. You thought I was going to *hit* you. That I was the kind of man who would hit a woman. Everyone in my life seems to think the worst of me. I get that. It is what it is." He sounded like he was having a big old pity party, and

131

truth be known, he was. He was just so tired of everyone thinking the worst of him. He'd always been polite, even gentle with her, but she thought he would *hit* her.

She rested a hand on his arm, but he ignored that, too. Well, he tried to ignore it.

"I don't. I just…" Her voice cracked.

That did make him turn to look at her. He could hear the raw pain in her voice.

"I saw your hand coming toward me, and I reacted like…" She shuddered and closed her eyes. After a moment, she opened them and looked directly at him. "I reacted like I was used to reacting. I dodged away so I wouldn't get hit again."

"Again?" His eyes narrowed, and he searched her face.

"I… Bobby's father… he…" Tears flooded her eyes, and she stopped, struggling to compose herself.

AJ looked at her closely, threw some bills on the bar, and stood up. "Come on. Let's go outside where we can talk."

She slid off the barstool and followed him out of The Lucky Duck.

"There, let's go to the gazebo." He pointed to the empty gazebo down at the end of Oak Street.

They walked silently down the sidewalk then

climbed the stairs to the gazebo. She leaned against the railing, so he did too, waiting for her to begin talking again.

He sensed more than heard her take in a big breath of air. "I left Bobby's father because he hit me. He hit me a lot. I finally got up enough nerve to leave him. I took Bobby, and we went on the road, hiding from Kurt."

His heart squeezed in his chest, and sympathy mingled with anger. "I'm so sorry. I had no idea." He raked his hand through his hair, feeling like a fool for making this about him after all she'd gone through.

"He found us, though. Here on the island." She turned and looked out toward the bay at the end of the walkway.

He swiveled around, looking down at her.

She continued but didn't look at him. "I should have left him sooner. I don't know why it took me so long. He said I made him do it. That if I didn't make him mad, it wouldn't happen. It sounds so silly when I say it now." She traced her finger along the top of the railing. "But when he got rough with Bobby... well, I knew we couldn't stay."

He let her take her time, telling her story on her own terms.

"When Kurt got here and found us, well... he

hit me again. But Eddie came and stopped him." She reached up to touch her face as if feeling Kurt's blows.

His heart twisted. She'd gone through so much. How could anyone hurt her like that?

"Anyway, the police came and took him away, so finally, Bobby and I were safe." She turned to him then. "But when your hand came flying past my face... I just instinctively ducked. I couldn't sort out the past from the present."

He reached out—ever so slowly—to touch her face. Her hand rose to meet his and pressed it against her cheek.

"I would never hit you. Ever. I'm sorry I scared you. So sorry I brought all this back up to you. And I'm so, so sorry I stormed out without letting you explain."

"I just wanted you to know I really didn't think *you* would hit me. It was all me. Just my messed up past making me react like that." Her voice was low and broke his heart in ways he wasn't prepared for.

He wiped away her tears then slowly pulled her into his arms to hold her against him. Letting her cry. Letting her feel his warmth and protection.

That Kurt guy better never show his face or... well, AJ made no promises about keeping himself out of the papers if the man ever showed up.

Courtney leaned against him, and he held her close, stroking her hair, trying to give her some of his strength.

Finally, she looked up at him and gave him a tentative look. "So, we're all good now?"

He wasn't sure he'd ever be *good* again. Not after hearing what had happened to Courtney. A fierce wave of protectiveness swept over him, too strong to deny. He reached out, painfully aware of how slowly he moved his hand, and tilted her chin up so he could look directly into her eyes. "Yes, things between us are fine."

As much as he wanted to kiss her at that moment, he knew the timing was all wrong. So he gently wrapped his arms back around her, and they both stood looking out over the water.

CHAPTER 14

"Momma, you're taking forever." Bobby danced from foot to foot. "Mr. Hamilton isn't gonna wait all day, you know."

"I have to finish packing the picnic lunch." Courtney peeked into the picnic basket. Sandwiches, chips, fresh fruit, and a jug of lemonade. She added a tin of cookies. She'd packed enough for a dozen people even though it would only be AJ, Bobby, and her.

AJ had surprised her when he asked if she wanted to go on a picnic today and include Bobby. She'd said yes if she could bring the food, since she wasn't sure that AJ was up on food six-year-old boys liked. Not that Bobby was a picky eater, but he did have his favorites.

"Do you have your swimsuit on under that? You said we could go in the ocean." Bobby eyed her.

She'd slipped on shorts and a t-shirt over her suit. "I do have it on. Go grab our beach bag."

Bobby raced over and picked up the bag with towels, flip-flops, and suntan lotion. "Hurry up. We want to be ready when Mr. Hamilton gets here."

She turned at the sound of a knock at the door. Before she'd even taken a step, Bobby had tugged the door open. "Hey, Mr. Hamilton. We're all ready. Well, Momma is almost ready. Girls take *forever* to get ready, don't they?"

AJ stepped inside and looked at her appreciatively. She self-consciously tucked a wisp of hair behind her ear. She'd be glad when it grew out enough to pull it back. "I'm ready, too."

AJ stepped aside and she and Bobby walked out the door.

"Oh, boy. Look at his car. It's a convertible. We're going to ride with the top down?" Bobby danced around in excitement.

"We sure are. You have to wear your seatbelt though."

"I always wear my seatbelt. Momma makes me."

"It's a good rule to have." AJ took the picnic basket from Courtney and placed it in the back seat. He leaned close to her and whispered, "You look very fetching today."

Fetching? Who said that anymore? But, somehow, it sounded just right coming from him. A warm blush crept over her face. He looked rather good himself. He'd gotten a haircut, and his thick, brown hair no longer had that slightly shaggy, in-need-of-a-trim look.

"Does Bobby need a car seat or something?"

"Yes, let me grab his booster seat from my car." She took Bobby's seat out of her car and fixed it in AJ's. Bobby climbed in and fastened up.

AJ opened the car door for her, and she slipped into the front seat. He climbed in and they headed off to Lighthouse Point. The wind tousled her hair into a wild mess, but she didn't mind. She felt carefree for the first time in a very long time. Riding along in the car with Bobby and AJ, the wind on their faces, seemed like a perfect way to spend a glorious afternoon.

AJ glanced over at Courtney. She looked beautiful with her hair tossing about and a wide smile on her face. She tilted her face to the sunshine. This was turning into a perfect day.

He pulled into the parking lot near Lighthouse Point. Bobby scampered out of the car. "We should hurry and get set up. Then we can go in the ocean, right, Momma?"

AJ grabbed the picnic basket then popped the trunk. Courtney looked inside and laughed. "You thought of everything, huh?"

"I wasn't sure what all we needed." He looked at the umbrella, beach blanket, and three chairs. "Overkill?"

"We could leave the chairs and just use the blanket. Come on, I'll help you carry it all." She took the beach blanket and her tote bag.

He balanced the umbrella on one shoulder and carried the basket in his other hand.

"Now, can we go?" Bobby skipped down the path to the beach.

They walked after him with their load. They found a spot near the lighthouse to spread out the blanket while Bobby raced down to the water.

"Just stay at the edge until I get down there with you," Courtney called out.

"I know, Momma. I know."

He wrestled the umbrella into submission. Kind of. It tilted crazily but cast a shadow across one edge of the blanket. Good enough. He placed the picnic basket in the shade.

"I should go let Bobby swim for a bit." Courtney slipped off her shorts and let them drop onto the blanket. With another swift movement, she tugged off her t-shirt and let it drop beside the shorts. She wore a bright blue two-piece swimsuit, and she looked… fabulous. Better than fabulous.

He shucked off his t-shirt. "I'm ready if you are."

They walked across the warm sand to the shoreline.

"Can I get in now?"

"Yes, I'm coming in with you."

He watched while Courtney waded out into the ocean, holding Bobby's hand. The gulf was calm today, with gently rolling waves. With a whoop, he raced into the water and swung his arm around in a large arc, splashing Bobby and Courtney. Bobby shrieked with laughter, held onto his mother's hands, lifted his feet, and kicked up a waterfall of water in AJ's direction. AJ responded with another good splash.

Bobby bobbed up by his mother's side. "I can swim. Wanna see me?" Without waiting for a reply, he swam the short distance to AJ and climbed onto his back. "Look, Momma. I'm tall now."

"Bobby, don't go climbing all over Mr. Hamilton."

"I don't mind." And he realized he didn't. He swam a bit with Bobby riding on his back then stood up and tossed Bobby up in the air. Bobby laughed and came splashing down beside him.

"Do it again."

He tossed Bobby up again and again until his arms grew weary. They all swam along the shore and splashed each other in a winner-takes-all water fight. Laughter punctuated the friendly battle. He grinned every time he heard her infectious laugh. They all finally waded to the shore, water running down their salty skin, and headed back to where they had spread out their things.

Bobby dropped down onto the blanket and grinned. "That was the most fun ever. Now I'm starving."

Courtney grabbed a towel and dried off a bit, then wrapped the towel around her waist. "I'll get the food ready."

He watched her, her hair glistening from the seawater, her cheeks rosy from the sun. He dried off some and dropped onto the blanket by Bobby.

Courtney had brought an impressive spread. Sandwiches of all kinds, cut fruit, chips, and cookies. "Wow, you know how to do a picnic."

"I wasn't sure what you liked… so I brought… um… a variety."

"I'll say."

"I want the peanut butter and jelly sandwich." Bobby reached for it.

"Bobby, our guest chooses first."

Bobby scowled. "Okay, but he better not pick the peanut butter and jelly one."

AJ smothered a grin. "I think I'll take the ham sandwich."

"Oh, good." Bobby reached for his sandwich.

Courtney poured them all lemonade, opened the bag of chips, and passed out napkins.

As he took a bite, AJ realized he'd worked up quite an appetite playing in the surf. The plain picnic was perfect. The last "picnic" he'd gone on had been on a yacht with a catered picnic basket with fancy-named appetizers and very expensive wine. This simple meal suited him much more, to his amazement. He wasn't sure what spell this island had cast over him—or maybe Courtney had cast a spell—but he'd grown to like more simple pleasures. And that surprised him very much.

"Can we go make a wish at the lighthouse now?" Bobby jumped up after consuming more food than AJ could believe a little kid could possibly eat.

"Let us finish our lunch first." Courtney

laughed. "You can go to the edge of the water and collect shells, but don't go in without us."

He raced to the shore.

"Does he ever run out of energy?" AJ watched the boy in amazement.

"Rarely. Though when he does, he drops off hard and fast."

"He seems like a great kid."

"He is." She smiled. "He's the best thing that ever happened to me."

"Can I ask you something?" He wasn't sure he should.

"Of course."

"Did he do okay when you were on the run from his father? Did he understand what was going on?"

She put down her drink. "He understood some of it. He'd seen Kurt hit me. He tried to stop Kurt one time, and Kurt flung him across the room."

"Tough life for such a little kid."

"It was. But now he has a stable place to live. He has Tally and Eddie. It's almost magical how it all fell into place. Like it was meant to be."

"Well, I'm glad it worked out the way it did for both of you." He was glad Courtney and Bobby were out of danger now and had found a family. He was even the tiniest bit jealous if that made any sense at all. Just a normal family life. What he wouldn't have given to have that.

Courtney stood. "Well, I better go let Bobby make his wish. You coming?"

"Sure." He jumped up and headed across the sand. They bumped against each other on the uneven surface, and he reached out to steady her. He was immediately afraid he'd moved too quickly, but she looked up and smiled at him. Her skin was warm and smooth beneath his touch. He lingered with his hand on her arm for a moment longer than needed.

Bobby raced up to them. "We need to go right by the lighthouse to make a wish. Come on." He grabbed AJ's hand and tugged.

AJ trotted down the beach after Bobby. When they reached the *exact* right spot—according to Bobby—he commanded them to find their shell for their wish.

Bobby prowled the shore, looking for the perfect shell.

Courtney leaned down and picked out a shell. "I don't really need to wish for anything. I have everything I could ever want." She closed her eyes anyway, paused, then tossed the shell into the ocean.

AJ didn't believe in this wish nonsense, but no

way was he going to disappoint Bobby. He leaned down and picked up a smooth shell tinged with yellow.

"Whatcha gonna wish for, Mr. Hamilton?"

"I'm not sure."

"Well, make it a good one." Bobby stood with his hand on one hip, watching him.

AJ couldn't think of anything to wish for, because this day was perfect. He'd love to have more days just like this. After a few moments' thought, still drawing a blank, he smiled at Bobby and tossed the shell into the sea. No need for the boy to know he hadn't made a wish.

"Now, I'm gonna make mine." Bobby squinted his eyes closed, his face a mask of concentration. He opened his eyes and flung the shell as far as his short arm would toss it. It plunked into the ocean.

"Well, I bet all our wishes come true." The boy grinned then tagged AJ. "You're it. Bet you can't catch me."

With a whoop, Bobby raced down the beach. AJ grinned at Courtney then raced after the boy.

CHAPTER 15

Courtney stood on the long porch in front of Magic Cafe and hugged her grandparents. "You both have a great time."

"I'm sure we will." Eddie draped his arm around Tally's shoulders.

"Are you sure you'll be okay here with the restaurant? It's not too much, too soon?" Tally's eyes clouded with worry.

"Absolutely not. I'll be fine. Tereza will help. You two just go and have fun."

"You'll call if you have any questions?"

"Yes, of course, I will." It would take a disaster the size of a category five hurricane for her to actually call and interrupt their getaway, but Tally didn't have to know that.

"I feel badly we're not here to help with Bobby, either."

"Tally, go. Bobby is spending the night with Stevie. I've got his care figured out for the whole weekend."

They got into Eddie's car, and she waved as they pulled away. She wanted to make Tally and Eddie proud. They'd done so much for her. She wanted to repay some of that. Three days. How much could she mess up in three days? She had everything under control. Everything.

She walked back into Magic Cafe. A loud crash sounded from the kitchen, and she hurried to see what was wrong.

A pot teetered on the floor with pieces of pasta strewn everywhere. "I'm sorry. I was picking it up and it just slipped from my hands," one of the cooks apologized.

"Did you get burned?" She quickly walked over.

"No, ma'am."

Courtney paused, not used to being called ma'am. Is that what happened when you were in charge of a business? "Well, I'm glad you're okay. Let's get another pot on, give a complimentary appetizer for anyone waiting on a pasta dish, and we'll get this mess cleaned up."

There, she'd handled her first problem. This wasn't going to be so hard.

She helped clean up the mess, dried everything as much as possible, and angled a fan across the floor to make sure it dried quickly. The last thing she needed was for someone to slip.

The door to the kitchen swung open. "Courtney, I'm so sorry." A new, young waitress was almost in tears. "I was getting drinks for table five, and the people at table three just slipped away without paying their bill."

Courtney closed her eyes for a moment. People. She couldn't believe people sometimes. She opened her eyes and smiled encouragingly to the new waitress. "That's okay. Try to keep a better watch, but these things happen."

The waitress looked at her gratefully, grabbed a tray of food, and headed back out to the deck.

Probably wasn't going to be their most profitable day if people left without paying, and she'd given out a half-dozen or so free appetizers. But, hey, the restaurant was still standing.

She went out to the deck, grabbed a waitress apron, and helped with the lunch crowd. Employees constantly came to her with questions as she tried to help deliver food and take orders. She wasn't sure she'd ever seen the restaurant this busy for so many hours. It figured it would happen just as Tally left. She didn't know how Tally always looked so cool and collected as she ran Magic Cafe. By dinnertime, Courtney was ready to scream in frustration, but she patiently answered questions and helped out in the kitchen as well as the restaurant.

She hadn't so much as sat down once for hours and hours. Her stomach growled in hunger, but she ignored it except for swiping two hushpuppies as she walked past a fresh batch in the kitchen. Time enough to eat after the crowd thinned. If it ever did.

So much for thinking this wouldn't be a profitable day. This was like the crowd that never ends.

AJ walked over to Magic Cafe about an hour before closing and sat at the bar. He was surprised by the number of patrons still there. Courtney threw him a hurried smile as she rushed past but didn't stop to talk. Damp ringlets of hair framed her face. Her cheeks were rosy red, and her eyes showed exhaustion. He looked out and saw several tables that needed to be cleared.

He jumped off his stool, grabbed a gray bin

from the cart in the corner, walked over, and started clearing a table while chatting nicely to the folks sitting there sipping their after-dinner coffee.

Courtney crossed over and placed a hand on his arm, stopping him. "You don't have to do that."

"Don't mind a bit. I'll just take these into the kitchen."

He walked into the kitchen and saw dirty dishes piling up in the corner by the dishwashing station. Without really thinking, he grabbed a handful and started the rinsing process. This was something he knew how to do. His father had insisted he work his way through every station at the restaurants before he'd gone into management. It had been quite the education.

Courtney pushed through the door, balancing a tray on her hip. "What are you doing?"

"Dishes?" He grinned at her, foamy bubbles dripping from his gloved hands.

She shook her head. "You don't—"

"I know. I don't have to. But I want to help. You look exhausted."

"Well, the new dishwasher guy we hired just walked out a couple of hours ago. Said it was too much work."

"I'll see if I can get some of these finished up. I know the drill."

"You do?" Her eyes narrowed.

"I kind of know a lot about restaurants."

"Well, I'm not going to say no, if you're sure. We can use the help. Otherwise, I'm going to be here all night right until we open again in the morning." She set the tray of dishes on the counter. "I better go out there and help Tereza."

He stayed at his post for a good hour, catching up the dishes. The steamy water made this corner of the kitchen feel like a sauna. His t-shirt stuck to him like a second skin.

Tereza finally walked in. "The last customer is gone. Let me finish those. Thanks for the help. We were swamped tonight." Her tone actually sounded grateful instead of accusatorial like the last few times he'd spoken to her. That's a step in the right direction.

"I can finish them up."

"Nah, you go find Courtney. I think she headed to Tally's office to close out the night."

He walked out of the kitchen and onto the deck. A cool breeze brought instant relief. He plucked at his t-shirt, releasing its sweaty glued-on suction, and ran his hand through his hair, relishing the fresh air. A few waiters were clearing the last of the tables. The blast of air-conditioned coolness smacked him as he wandered inside to find Courtney.

Courtney shoved her hair away from her face and looked at the scratched notes she'd taken on how to close out the day. She thought she'd had it all written down, but something wasn't working. The totals didn't equal, and she had no idea where to start to figure it out. She wanted to bang her hands on the keyboard but didn't think that would solve anything.

She turned at the sound of someone entering the office. "AJ, you're still here."

"I am. I thought I'd check on you before I left."

She leaned back in her chair. "I'm trying to close out the day but not having much luck."

"What software package are you using?"

She looked at him, surprised at his question. "Tally just got this new system that integrates almost everything. It's called…" She glanced at the computer screen. "Restaurant Plus."

"Perfect. Let me help you." He pulled a chair up next to her. "I know that system."

"You do?"

He shrugged. "It's kind of… well, my father and

uncle own a company that developed this software and one for hotel management."

"Really?" There was so much about this man that she had no clue about. She looked at him closely, seeing a hint of avoidance in his eyes. "And how do you know so much about working in a restaurant? You seemed right at home tonight."

"Oh, that." He shrugged like it was no big deal, but she wasn't fooled. "My father owns a couple chains of restaurants."

"Which ones?" She pinned him with her gaze.

He hesitated and shifted in his seat. "Bistro Fifty."

"I hear those are really nice."

"And he does all the fancy restaurants at the Hamilton Hotels, too. Plus he has some trendy wine bars."

"Wow."

"So, anyway, I worked my way through different jobs at lots of the restaurants. So, you could say restaurants are in my blood, just like you." He picked up some papers she'd put on the desk, efficiently changing the subject. "Here, let me see what you have."

They worked side by side with AJ patiently explaining what he was doing. Within fifteen minutes, they were finished. She reached up and stretched her arms high above her head. "Now that was a long day."

"I'm sure it was. The restaurant was hopping tonight."

"Yes. Yes, it was. And I'm so ready for bed."

Tereza poked her head in the door. "I'm going to close up. I need about twenty more minutes to get the kitchen back into shape. Why don't you go on home?"

"You sure?" She felt like she should be the last to leave.

"I'm sure." Tereza grinned. "You know I'd rather close than open. You've got to open in the morning, right? And I'll be in right before the lunch shift."

"Okay, thanks." She slowly stood, all her muscles screaming at her.

AJ rose beside her. "Can I walk you home?"

"You don't have to."

"You keep saying that to me. I'm offering to do things because I want to. So just say yes." He winked at her and tossed her his charming boyish smile.

The smile that made her heart flip and her pulse race. "Yes."

They walked out into the fresh evening air. She took in a deep breath. Stars twinkled overhead, and the palm fronds moved just slightly in the night breeze. They headed down the sidewalk, and she looked down in surprise when AJ took her hand in his. He squeezed it and smiled at her. This time, it wasn't his regular charming smile. It was one filled with ease and companionship.

They walked on in silence. Exhaustion coursed through her in constant waves, beating on her so unendingly she could hardly carry on a coherent conversation. How did Tally do this day after day?

They got to her bungalow, and she unlocked the door. "Thank you for all your help today. I really appreciate it."

"You're welcome." He smiled at her. "You should go inside before you fall asleep on your feet."

"I am tired." She leaned against the doorframe.

"I'll see you tomorrow. I'll come by and see how things are going at Magic Cafe." His lips curled up into a grin, and he pointed his finger at her in a mock display of chewing her out. "And don't say I don't have to."

She grinned then, too, and watched as he walked away and headed back to his rental. Once again, a shiver ran up her spine. Frowning, she glanced around the courtyard to the other bungalows. She didn't know why she was being so ridiculous.

She slipped inside and closed the door firmly

behind her. After locking it, she turned out the low light. Just to prove to herself she wasn't creeped out, she walked back to her bedroom in the darkness.

Courtney threw herself on the bed and kicked off her shoes, sure if she tried to get back up and slip out of her clothes, she would just drop to the floor in exhaustion. She rolled over and closed her eyes, forgetting about the eerie feeling.

CHAPTER 16

The next morning, Delbert stood in the open doorway to AJ's room. "May I come in? Granice said you were up here."

AJ thought briefly about saying no and closing the door on Delbert, but he was in an unusually great mood this morning after his evening with Courtney. Not even his family could squash his cheeriness. He motioned for his cousin to come in.

"I've tried texting and calling. You didn't answer." Delbert walked into the room. "I wanted to tell you how sorry I am. I reacted badly. I shouldn't have assumed you were at the middle of the ruckus at the club."

AJ didn't say a word.

"I'm becoming too like our fathers. A quick

judgment before I know all the facts. I'm really sorry. Let's not let my stupid mistake mess up our friendship. You're the only cousin I actually enjoy being around." Delbert laughed.

AJ grinned in spite of himself and reached out a hand. "Okay. Truce."

Delbert shook his hand. "I am sorry though. It was insensitive of me and just… wrong."

"Kind of like hearing you were wrong. You wanna say it again?"

"I was wrong," Delbert repeated himself good-naturedly. "We're all good?"

"We're good."

"So, Granice says you've been hiding out up here most of the week when you're even here. She thinks you're seeing someone."

"I'm not." He tossed out a small laugh. "Well, I am kind of."

"Tally's granddaughter?"

AJ looked at him in surprise. "How did you know?"

"I've known you for years. I saw the way you looked at her. Glancing around the restaurant to see where she was. I'd even go so far as to say you're smitten by her."

"Smitten? Who says that?"

"Me." Delbert crossed over and looked out the

window. "Nice view. And you didn't deny you were smitten, by the way."

"I'm just… well, heck, I don't know what I am." He went to stand by his cousin at the window. "I've enjoyed my time with her. She's… different. I even went on a picnic with her and her son."

"Bobby? He's a kick, isn't he?"

"Camille's not his biggest fan." AJ shook his head.

"Ah, Camille. She's just not used to being around kids."

"Well, I'm not either, but the boy is sure growing on me."

Delbert shook his head. "Yep, smitten."

Courtney looked over at table six, making sure they all had their food after the new waitress had spilled the entire tray with their order. Courtney had quickly put in a replacement order and comped the meal, along with apologizing for the delay. Luckily they were good sports about it, ordered another round of beers, and sat chatting while their meals were cooked again. Now they were happily eating their food.

Stevie's mother had brought Bobby by after

lunch, and he sat in the kitchen, mostly bored. He did have a few activity books and did a good job keeping himself occupied, but she felt bad for him. Not that she had a choice because she didn't have any other childcare options for him. He was supposed to have gone to his friend Mikey's to play, but Mikey had gotten sick.

"Everything going okay here?"

She turned at the sound of AJ's voice and couldn't help the immediate smile that crept across her face.

"Mr. Hamilton! Do you want to play? I have to stay here while Momma works, but it's not very fun." Bobby jumped up, rushed over to AJ, and tugged on AJ's hand.

"I… uh…"

"Bobby, it's not Mr. Hamilton's job to keep you entertained."

"But I'm a really fun player guy. I know lots of stuff we can play. Like alien invasion or maybe it could be the day the *starfish* invade the earth and we save it."

Confusion plastered itself across AJ's face and refused to budge. He looked helplessly at her.

"Bobby has an active imagination. He dreams up quite the games to play."

"So, do you wanna play? Huh?" Bobby hopped from foot to foot and stared up at AJ.

She almost felt sorry for AJ, he was so out of his element, but she couldn't help secretly being amused that a six-year-old boy could scare a grown man.

AJ thought of himself as a brave enough man… but why did the thought of spending an afternoon alone with Bobby scare him half to death?

"Sure, I'm up for it if you are." It was kind of a lie. He wasn't sure he'd be able to keep the boy safe, let alone entertained. What would they do? Shouldn't a person go to parenting class or something before they were asked to watch a kid? He turned to Courtney. "Mind you, I've never babysat a kid before in my life."

"I'm not a baby." Bobby puffed up his chest.

"See, I've already got it wrong."

"You'll do fine. You guys can play on the beach, go for ice cream, you could even go to the bungalow and play video games."

"Really?" Bobby's eyes lit up. "You hardly ever let me play video games."

"Special rules for today only." Courtney looked at AJ closely. "You sure you're up for this? You sure you want to do this?"

"I thought we had a conversation about I wouldn't offer to do things if I didn't want to do them." He just wasn't sure he wouldn't totally screw this one up.

"I know, but…"

"I'm sure." He wasn't sure at all but wasn't going to let her know that. He'd keep Bobby alive and unharmed… hopefully.

"I'm off about eight or nine. Tereza is going to close. I have a frozen pizza in the freezer you guys could have for dinner but don't give him a cola with dinner. Too much caffeine. His bedtime is eight."

"Can't I stay up until you get home?"

"Okay, just this once. We're not going to make a habit about staying up late, though."

AJ tried to keep it all straight. Video games were okay—but just today, not always. Something about an alien invasion on the beach—or had Bobby said *starfish* invasion? What was that? Ice cream yes, soda no.

Now was not the time to panic. He could do this.

Probably?

"Well, let's go, kiddo, and let your mom get back to work. What do you want to do first?"

"Let's go play space invaders. We'll both be good guys, and we'll have pretend bad guys."

Courtney grinned. "Have fun saving the world."

Bobby tugged his hand, and they headed off for the beach. How long could Bobby be out in the sun? He'd forgotten to ask. What other rules had he not even thought to question Courtney about? He looked down at Bobby's small hand in his, and the responsibility for another human being loomed over him.

He had to get this right.

"Come on. The invaders are here."

AJ was surprised he actually had fun playing Bobby's intricate game of space invaders which somehow morphed into starfish invaders and back to invaders from the Planet of Bad Guys. They played until he figured it was time to let Bobby rest. Okay, let *himself* rest. "How about we go get some ice cream?"

Bobby halted in his make-believe laser chase with a particularly tenacious alien. "Ice cream is good." He dropped his laser-stick onto the beach and turned to take AJ's hand.

AJ was almost getting used to being tugged

around by him. The boy stopped in his tracks and frowned.

"What's wrong?" AJ looked toward where Bobby was staring at a group of palm trees and sea grapes lining the edge of the beach.

"I... I just thought I saw someone."

AJ didn't see anyone. "I got nothing, buddy. Who did you see?"

"I thought I saw... but it can't be him." His small face screwed up in confusion. "Nah, I guess it was nobody." Bobby took one last look toward the trees then tugged AJ's hand yet again.

He figured it was just part of the boy's active imagination. Maybe another space pirate or something of that ilk was creeping along the tree line.

"Come on. Let's get some ice cream. I want a *banilla* cone."

They got their ice cream then headed back to Courtney's bungalow. He took out the key she'd given him and opened the door. The cool air-conditioned air wrapped around him in a soothing, welcoming hug. He glanced around the apartment. The boxes that had been there the last time he visited were gone from the corners of the room. Courtney had hung up a photo of Tally, Eddie, Bobby, and her. A serene painting of a seascape hung on another wall. A small shelf filled with books and knickknacks sat against another wall.

The place was beginning to look like a home. Or what he imagined a normal home would look like. The huge house he'd been raised in had been decorated by an interior designer. A man's man house, she'd called it. They'd moved there about a year after his mother had died, leaving behind all remnants of his memories of happy times in the cheery house they'd lived in with his mom.

"Come on. Let's play some video games. I can't believe Momma said I can play them as much as we want today."

They played video games for an hour or so until Bobby announced he was hungry. AJ managed to cook the pizza without burning it and remembered to say no when Bobby asked for a soda with his dinner. He was almost getting cocky about how well he'd managed his responsibilities so far.

He looked at the time. Seven o'clock. Reinforcements would be here soon. Though, he actually was having a good time with the kid. Who knew? He was pretty certain his father had never spent a full afternoon and evening playing with him. Not even once in his whole life.

"More video games?" Bobby eyed him from across the table, his short legs perpetually swinging as he sat in his chair. The kid was in constant motion.

"How about I read you a book?"

"Really? That's cool. I've got a million books. Momma reads to me all the time. I'm learning to read."

"Okay then. Let's get this mess cleaned up, and we'll read."

Bobby helped him clear the table and put the dishes in the dishwasher. "The plates go like this, and you're supposed to put the silverware in upside down. I don't know why, but you do." Bobby's little shoulders went up and down, and the look on his face clearly said he thought his mother was a bit picky, but he wasn't going to break her dishwasher rules.

"Good to know." He reached down, grabbed the fork he'd put in, and turned it tines up.

Bobby grabbed a stack of books from the shelf, and they settled on the couch. He helped Bobby read a short book, but then Bobby wanted him to read a chapter book about a boy who found a hidden treasure chest. Bobby curled up next to him, resting his head on AJ's arm. He looked down after just reading a few pages when he realized Bobby had quit asking questions.

And just like that, the boy was sound asleep.

He closed the book but was afraid to move, afraid he'd wake Bobby. He sat there, listening to the boy's soft, even breathing. It was one of the most peaceful moments he'd ever had in his life.

And that scared him half to death.

CHAPTER 17

Courtney walked through the door of the bungalow a little after eight. She stopped in her tracks, and a small smile crept across her face. AJ was sound asleep on the couch with Bobby curled up against him. Her heart fluttered in her chest. She stood and drank in the scene and the pure serenity of it.

When she closed the door behind her, AJ's eyes opened. He gave her a lazy grin as she tiptoed over to the couch.

"Has he been out long?" she asked.

AJ glanced at the clock on the wall. "About an hour. I was afraid to move. Afraid I'd wake him up."

"I should have warned you. Once he's out, he's out. You can pick him up, carry him, and he doesn't even wake up."

She leaned over to pick Bobby up.

"Here, I'll get him." AJ gently turned, scooped the boy up in his arms, and stood with one easy motion.

She led the way down the hallway and into Bobby's room. AJ carefully set him on the bed. She tugged off her son's shorts and slipped him under the covers. Smiling, she bent down and kissed his cheek. He looked just like an angel when he slept. No sign of the constant whirl of activity that followed him all day long.

AJ leaned down and brushed a lock of Bobby's hair away from his face in a slow, gentle movement. Her heart flipped in her chest at the simple sight.

"Night, kiddo," he whispered.

They left the bedroom, their soft footsteps in sync as they walked down the hall.

AJ stood for a moment in the middle of the front room. "I guess I should go now." But his eyes said he wanted to stay.

She could see it plainly. And since when did she know what his eyes said? "Do you want to stay for a bit? I could use some time to unwind."

"Sure, I can stay." His eyes lit up, and she liked that. Liked that a lot.

"Get you a beer?"

"Sure."

She headed to the kitchen, but he followed after her.

She got him a beer and a tall glass of ice water for herself. She felt him watch her every move. The tension in the air crackled between them. Did he feel that?

He moved closer to her and reached for the drinks. He carefully set them both on the counter. "Court?"

"Hmm?" She watched his eyes as they burned into her.

"I'd really like to kiss you."

She swallowed, uncertain if she was ready for this step. Kurt had done such a number on her. Made it so she didn't really trust men. But AJ wasn't men. AJ was... AJ. And she trusted him. She knew in her heart she trusted him. She swept her gaze over his face and locked on his eyes. Yes, yes, she was ready for this. She nodded. "I'd like that, too." Her words were barely over a whisper.

He slowly lowered his lips against hers. A thrill of emotions rolled through her, and she didn't have time to sort them all out.

He pulled away. "And another one?"

She nodded.

He kissed her again, this time a long, leisurely kiss that left her breathless. When he finally pulled away, he picked up their drinks and handed hers to her. He took her hand in his and led her back to the couch. He sat down, pulling her close beside him.

She watched as he took a long swallow of his beer, his strong hand wrapped around the bottle. Taking a slow breath, she forced herself to look away. She couldn't just sit and stare at him forever, could she?

She pressed the cool glass of water to her lips, the chill a sharp contrast to the fire of his kisses. Ignoring all thoughts of his kiss, she took a quick swallow.

Talk. They should talk. She turned to him, trying not to stare at his lips again. "So, tell me about you. You know a lot about me, my family. You don't say much about your life or your family. All I know is your father owns restaurants."

He set his beer down carefully on a coaster. "There's not much to tell. I have a father who lives in Washington, DC. My grandmother lives there, too. But, as you know, I'm staying here with her at her rental. I…" He paused for so long she wasn't sure he was going to continue.

"I was actually banished here. My father is ticked off at me."

"Banished you?"

"I used to work for him, but we had a falling

out. I've been… well, I haven't been doing much of anything the last few years. Just traveling around. Hanging out with friends."

"You haven't worked?" The concept of not working just boggled her mind.

"Nope."

"But how do you live? I mean…" Embarrassment raced through her. She'd almost asked him what he did for money, which was none of her business.

He looked at her and shrugged. "I'm a trust fund baby and have access to some of the funds now, much to my father's dismay. He'd rather me be penniless, but my great-grandfather set up these trusts, and, well, I can access some of the money, but not the rest until I turn forty."

She still couldn't quite wrap her mind around not ever working. Just having money to spend on anything you wanted without earning it. A different lifestyle for sure.

"I mainly haven't gotten another job because it irritates my father to see me not work. And I find a bit of joy in annoying him." He picked up his beer and took a swallow. "I know it sounds shallow, but he's… well, he's a tough one. I can't ever do right in his mind, so I've pretty much quit trying."

"Why is his opinion so important?"

He looked at her and did one of his long pauses again. She sat waiting for him to continue... or tell her to mind her own business.

"Honestly, I don't know. My whole life I tried, I really did. I'd get straight As in high school, and he'd be mad I wasn't first in my class. I'd score a goal in lacrosse, and he'd be disappointed because someone else on the team scored two. I've never been able to measure up to whatever it is he wants me to be."

"Maybe you should quit trying."

"I should, but it's a habit that's hard to break."

"How about your mother? What does she say?"

"My mother is dead. She died when I was six. My whole world turned upside down that year."

"That must have been so hard."

"It was. She was my biggest supporter. I remember her smile. She smiled a lot. And laughed. We lived in this big, sunny house. But then... she was gone. We found out she had cancer, and she was gone in months. My father sold the house, and he and I moved to a cold, sterile house. We never talked about my mother." He shrugged as if it was no big deal, but she could see in his eyes how much this all still haunted him.

She put her hand on his hand resting on the couch, trying to connect with him, trying to say to that little boy who lost his mother, without words, that everything would be okay. She'd never known her own mother, but would it be worse to know your mom and lose her? Both were horrible things to happen to any child, and it tore at her heart.

"Anyway, I made the gossip page of the paper one time too many. My father sent me away with my grandmother, threatening to find a way to cut me off. I wouldn't put it past him. He's ruthless. My mother was the only one who could bring out a softer side of him."

"I'm sorry."

"Don't be. I'll be fine. I've always been fine. I always find a way to land on my feet. I'll do my penance and get back to my own life." He shrugged again. "Or he'll cut me off, and I'll move on."

AJ looked at Courtney. He could see pity in her eyes, and he didn't want that. He'd also seen the surprise when he said he didn't work. It was getting embarrassing, even to him, that he still hadn't found another job. It was getting tiring not working just to irritate his father. After seeing how hard Courtney worked and seeing the joy that owning Magic Cafe brought to Tally, his drift-through-life approach was beginning to lose its appeal.

He swooped his beer off the table and took a long swallow. Just like that, it was decided. He was going to start looking for a new job on Monday. But first, tomorrow he was going to help Courtney in any way she'd let him. He knew she was a bit overwhelmed with Tally being gone.

"So, how about I watch Bobby again tomorrow? We had a good time."

"I couldn't ask you—" She stopped and grinned at him. "But I didn't ask."

"So, that's a yes?"

"If you're sure. I was going to bring him into work early tomorrow with me and feed him breakfast there."

"How about I just come here? I'll pick up something for breakfast on the way. We'll just hang out all day."

"I'm sure Bobby would love that."

"It's settled then." He reluctantly stood though he really, really wanted to just sit by her side for hours more. "I should go. It's getting late, and I know you have another long day ahead of you tomorrow with Tally gone."

He reached down, and she slipped her small hand into his. Her hand was delicate and warm. He deftly pulled her to her feet. She bumped against him, and he circled his arm around her waist. He tilted her head up and kissed her. He'd been wanting to do it again, ever since they sat down on the couch.

A small sigh escaped her lips. He tightened his hold on her, pressing her closer. She finally pulled away, a small, shy smile on her face.

He cleared his throat. "Yes, I should go." He released his hold, and she stepped back, leaving an empty loneliness in her place.

She walked him to the door and opened it. He leaned in for one more quick kiss and then started across the courtyard. Partway to the street, he looked back and waved. She returned the wave then closed the door. A crunching sound across the courtyard caught his attention, but when he looked, he didn't see a thing.

He turned and headed down the street, whistling a random love song as he ambled along the sidewalk. A fleeting thought entered his mind. He could almost imagine himself in a life like this. Picnics on the beach, family dinners, quiet evenings.

Ah, but that was silly... wasn't it?

CHAPTER 18

AJ balanced a tray with two coffees and a sack of delicious-smelling baked goods from The Sweet Shoppe as he knocked on the door to Courtney's bungalow.

She answered after a moment, and he almost dropped his packages when she flashed him an I'm-so-glad-to-see-you smile. He wanted to kiss her but had no idea if Bobby was watching and how she'd feel about that. Instead, he simply said, "Good morning."

"Come in. Bobby's still sleeping."

He instantly regretted not kissing her and considered whether he could sneak one in now.

She stepped back and motioned for him to come in. He set the tray and sack down on a table and handed her one of the coffees. "Thought you could use this before work."

"Thank you." She took the offered cup. "I didn't have time to make a pot this morning. I try and grab some at work, but this is wonderful. I'll drink it on my walk to the restaurant."

"There's cream in the bag if you need it."

"Nope, just black, thanks." She looked around the room. "Got to find my purse and get out of here. Bobby should be up soon. Oh, there it is." She crossed over, picked up her purse, and hurried back to the door. "I've really got to go. Thanks for the coffee." Her words were like one long stream of consciousness.

"Go. We'll be fine."

She slipped out the door, and the sudden silence of the apartment unnerved him. An emptiness flooded the room like she'd sucked away the life, oxygen, and sunlight.

He shook his head. He was becoming a crazy man. As he picked up the sack of baked goods, he realized he hadn't offered her one. Well, she'd probably grab something to eat at Magic Cafe.

He crossed to the kitchen and set the sack on the counter. The sound of small, quiet footsteps drew his attention to the doorway.

Bobby stood there, rubbing his eyes. "Hey, Mr. Hamilton. You're here."

"I told your mom we'd hang out again today while she works. That okay with you?"

The boy's eyes brightened. "You bet. We can go to the beach and play invaders again and maybe to Lighthouse Point and make a wish and did Momma say I could play video games again?"

He could see Bobby had inherited his mother's stream of consciousness conversation. "How about you go get dressed?" Did he need help? Would Bobby be offended if he asked if he needed help?

"Okay. I'll be right back."

The sound of his feet padding down the hall was comforting after the quietude when Courtney left. Bobby was back within minutes, dressed in shorts and a t-shirt.

"Hey, buddy. Shirt's on backward."

Bobby ducked his head and stared at the shirt. He let out one of his long sighs. The sighs that were amazingly long for such a little kid, but AJ was getting used to them. "I was hurrying." He struggled to wiggle out of the shirt, and AJ went over to give him a hand.

"There. Now, how about some breakfast?"

"I'm starving."

AJ put the baked goods on a plate and poured Bobby a glass of milk.

"I can't decide which one to pick. I like Miss Julie's cinnamon rolls, but that one there with the chocolate looks good."

"Have them both?"

"Really?" His eyes got wide.

AJ realized he'd probably made a mistake. "Would your mother let you have both?"

"Nah." Another long sigh.

"Well, how about if we cut them in half and you have a half of each one?"

"Hey, that works."

He watched while Bobby inhaled his breakfast. The kid could eat, he'd give him that. Bobby finished off the milk and swiped a hand across his mouth. "Now we gotta go play."

"I'm sure we do." AJ got up to clear the table.

"But first I have to go brush my teeth. Momma says I have to every morning after breakfast. Every one. Moms have a lot of rules."

"They do." He nodded gravely, trying to hide a grin.

Bobby came back in a few minutes. "Can we go to the beach? The real beach, not the bay, the ocean beach."

"Okay, we can do that." He took one last look

around to make sure he hadn't left a mess for Courtney to deal with, and they headed out the door.

For the first part of the walk, Bobby stopped at each crack in the sidewalk and made an exaggerated leap over it. "I don't wanna break Momma's back."

"What?"

"Step on a crack, you break your mother's back." Bobby looked at him like he was a clueless alien. And maybe he was to this world of kids and playing and, well, everything.

They got to the beach and played attack of the starfish invaders. Then alien invasion. Then some strange mix of the two. He couldn't quite figure out what was going on but did what Bobby commanded and was pretty sure he saved the world a time or two.

"How about a snow-cone? Does that sound good?" He needed a break, and food was as good a way to get Bobby's attention as any. "There's a snow-cone stand just back that way." He pointed down the beach to a row of small shops.

They crossed to the boardwalk at the edge of the beach and headed toward the shops. When they were almost there, Bobby stopped. "I'm gonna stand here at this walkway and watch out for aliens."

185

AJ eyed the distance from the arched walkway to the beach and the shops. He'd still be able to see Bobby. "Okay, but don't go any further than this."

"I'll be watching for the bad guys so we can beat them again after we have our snow-cones. I want a red one, no, purple, no, red."

"Red it is." AJ trotted over to the snow-cone booth and stood in line. He kept an eye on Bobby as the line moved forward. When he got to the front, he ordered two snow-cones and pulled out his wallet. He paid for the cones and turned back to the arched walkway.

Bobby wasn't standing there at the top like before. He hurried over and climbed the walkway. "Bobby." He looked both directions. "Bobby, where are you?"

There was absolutely no sign of the boy. AJ hurried onto the beach and stopped a couple standing at the end of the walkway. "Have you seen a little boy? Red t-shirt? About six?"

They shook their heads. His heart began to pound in his chest, and he dropped the snow-cones into the trashcan at the edge of the beach. He took off at a run to the water's edge and looked both directions. "Bobby." The wind buffeted his call.

Turning in circles, AJ ran his hands through his hair. What had he done? Where was Bobby? Why had he let the boy wait on the walkway instead of holding firmly to his hand every single second?

He hurried back to the walkway, up and over its arch over the dunes, and stood on the boardwalk, looking first to the left, then the right.

Nothing. No Bobby.

With his pulse racing and his mind whirling, he tugged out his phone and dialed Courtney.

"Hey, how goes the playday?" Her cheerful voice came across the airways.

"Court. I can't find him. He's just… gone."

"What do you mean, gone?" Courtney's heart crunched in her chest, her voice rising in a panicked crescendo. Tereza looked over at her, frowned, and hurried over.

"We played on the beach. I went to get snow-cones. He was standing right here. On the walkway to the beach… at the top of the arch over the dunes. I could see him from the snow-cone stand. But then I turned and he was just… gone."

"The snow-cone stand by Manchester Avenue?" She swallowed, trying to think of where there were snow-cone stands on the beach.

"I… I don't know."

"Look around. Tell me what you see."

"There are some shops. Terry's T-shirts and a place called As Luck Would Have It."

"Got it. Stay there, keep looking. I'll be there as fast as I can." She slid the phone into her shorts. "I've got to go. Bobby is missing."

"Go, go. I've got this." Tereza shooed her out of the restaurant.

Courtney ran out the door and debated whether it would be faster to race home and get her car or just run to where AJ and Bobby were. *Bobby had been.* She wheeled around and ran down the sidewalk, hoping it was quicker just to run there than double back for the car.

Each block seemed like a mile as she sped down the street, watching for Bobby as she raced by. She got to Manchester Avenue and cut over to the boardwalk.

AJ stood on the boardwalk looking in every direction, his face ashen. She raced up to him. "No sign?"

"None. I just turned for a minute, really. Just enough to order the snow-cones and pay for them. And he was gone. I don't know why he left that spot. He said he was watching for bad guys—aliens —why would he leave?" Fear and panic flooded AJ's eyes.

She paused for a moment and looked both directions. He wouldn't just leave. He'd run off one time, but that was because Stormy was missing and he wanted to help find him. This didn't make any sense.

"Courtney." She whirled around at the sound of her name. Eddie and Tally came running up to her.

"We got to Magic Cafe, and Tereza said Bobby was missing." Eddie held Tally's hand, her face pale and eyes filled with worry.

"It's my fault. I only turned around for a minute, but I should never have even let go of his hand." Regret and anguish ricocheted across AJ's face.

"Let's split up and look for him." Eddie took charge. "Tally and I will look along the beach. AJ, you look up and down the boardwalk. Courtney, why don't you head back to the bungalow, just in case he ended up there. Let me give you my phone number."

AJ handed Eddie his phone, and Eddie tapped in his number. AJ texted him back so Eddie would have his.

"I'm going to call the sheriff." Tally took out her phone.

AJ reached out and touched Courtney's hand. "I'm so, so sorry."

189

She just nodded, unable to give him the consolation he needed, only concerned about Bobby for now.

AJ turned and walked briskly down the boardwalk.

"I'm headed to the apartment. I'll call if he's there." She hoped he was there, though she couldn't imagine him just wandering away from AJ like that. She sped off down the street and cut across the island to the bungalow.

She looked left and right as she ran, hoping to catch a glimpse of Bobby. Nothing. No sign of him. Her heart thundered in her chest so loud she could barely catch a breath.

Bobby.

Oh, Bobby.

She reached the bungalow and pushed open the door, her heart rising when she noticed the door wasn't locked. He was here!

"Hello, Courtney."

She froze in her tracks, an icy fear coursing through her veins.

"Kurt."

"Momma?" Bobby's frightened voice filtered across the room from where he stood, Kurt's hand clasped onto Bobby's shirt, keeping him plastered firmly against Kurt's side.

Not again. No, please, not again.

Courtney darted her glance to the left and the right. She couldn't see anything to defend herself. She tried to send Bobby an encouraging look. "Bobby, it's okay."

"Not really," Kurt's words mocked her.

"What do you want, Kurt?" She debated throwing out the fact there was a restraining order against him but didn't want to aggravate him.

"You got a nice place here. Really nice." There was not a trace of pleasant chit-chat in his tone. "I'm thinking you have money now. And I'm thinking I deserve some of it."

"Sure. I can write you a check."

"Do you think I'm a fool?" He took a step closer, dragging Bobby with him. "I want cash."

Her phone rang, and she glanced down at it. She had two missed calls from Eddie, and this was AJ.

"Hand me the phone." His voice was threatening.

She grasped the phone tightly then looked at him. She reluctantly loosened her grip and handed him the phone, feeling as if she were lost at sea and he'd yanked the last life jacket out of her reach.

Kurt glanced at the phone. "Who's AJ? Is that the guy I saw you kissing the other night?"

191

A shiver ran up her spine. He'd been watching her. She'd sensed it. She should have done something about it instead of ignoring it.

"Momma, you kissed Mr. Hamilton?" Bobby's eyes shone with fear and now confusion.

She had to get Bobby away from Kurt.

And she knew one sure way to do it...

CHAPTER 19

AJ couldn't beat himself up any more if he tried. How could he lose Bobby? Why, oh why, had he let the boy stand on the walkway? A normal adult would have known not to let him stand that far from him. Kids wander off. Anyone with half a brain knew that. *He* should have known that. Who knew what space alien caught Bobby's attention and he raced after him.

Or it could be worse. Maybe Bobby didn't just wander off…

AJ's father was right. He was just one colossal screwup. Just one mistake after the next.

He methodically went into every single shop along the boardwalk, asking if anyone had seen Bobby and flashing his phone with a photo of the boy Eddie had sent him.

No one had seen Bobby.

He reached the end of the boardwalk and strode over one of the arching walkways to the beach, looking as far as he could in either direction, but no little boy in a red shirt.

He turned around to walk down the boardwalk again then paused. Should he try somewhere else? His mind whirled with indecision, which wasn't helping anyone.

He grabbed his phone and called Courtney. Five rings seemed like an eternity, but she didn't answer. Maybe she was talking to Eddie and Tally. Maybe they'd found him. He tapped off the phone then stood staring down at it, willing it to ring.

He almost dropped it when it did ring, and he looked at the phone number.

Eddie.

"Hello?" *Please, please say you've found Bobby.*

"Any luck?" Eddie's question dashed his hopes.

"No."

"I tried Courtney, but she's not answering." Eddie's voice took on an even more urgent concern than before.

"I tried, too." It was strange she wouldn't answer either of them. He would have thought she'd be right on top of the phone, waiting for word on

Bobby. "I could go to the bungalow and check on her."

"I think you should. We're way down the beach now. You're closer." Eddie's words were tense. "And, AJ?"

"Yes?"

"I'm beginning to fear we might have a problem with Courtney's ex, Kurt. There's a restraining order, but…"

"I'm on it. I'll get there as fast as I can."

He shoved his phone in his pocket and took off at a dead run toward the bungalow. No way was Kurt going to hurt Courtney again.

"Kurt, you know there's a restraining order against you." Courtney moved ever so slightly to the side.

"You think that would stop me?" He let out an ugly laugh that chilled her to her very bones. "You don't get to win. You don't get to live this perfect life while I rot in jail from your stupid charges against me." He took another step closer.

Which was exactly what she wanted. He needed to come close enough so she could grab Bobby away from him. Get him angry enough so he would focus on her and let go of Bobby.

"You're going to give me money. Lots of money. Cash. Then I'm gonna disappear somewhere you'll never find me." He sent her a self-satisfied smirk. "But you'll always be looking over your shoulder, won't you? Thinking I might be coming back for you. Back for Bobby."

"I'm not giving you a dime." She squared her shoulders and tried to sound strong and determined. She was astonished her words didn't come out as a hollow squeak.

All she could think of was keeping Bobby safe.

Kurt pulled Bobby by his collar and charged right up to her. "Yes, you are. Or I'm disappearing with Bobby, and you'll never see him again."

"Momma." Bobby's voice was filled with terror. "I don't wanna go with him."

"Okay, okay. You can have money. That's fine." She watched while Kurt relaxed his grip on Bobby's shirt. "I could go to the bank. Get cash. You could come with me so you can see I'm not talking to anyone. You can keep my phone."

Kurt looked like he was considering it.

"You could leave Bobby here."

"He'd call for help."

"No, he wouldn't. Not if I told him not to." Which she knew was a daring lie, but Kurt didn't have to know that. She sent a warning glance to Bobby.

"I want twenty-five thousand dollars."

"I don't have that much."

"You're lying. I know that old lady owns Magic Cafe. And that man who got the cops to arrest me. I know they're your family. They got money. I need the cash to get away from this mess you've made of my life."

"Okay, I lied. I have that much." If she kept him talking, maybe he wouldn't realize it was Sunday and the bank was closed because she couldn't bear to think of what would happen if Kurt stayed here all night waiting for the bank to open in the morning.

"I knew you were a dirty little liar."

She watched while history repeated itself and his arm snaked up and he wound up to slap her. As he concentrated on her, she reached out, grabbed Bobby, and shoved him toward the door. "Run."

Kurt's slap resounded across her cheek. The familiar sting. The instant pain. The automatic tears it brought to her eyes.

But that was okay. Bobby was out of Kurt's reach now, and the man had turned his total focus on her.

The door of the bungalow flew open, and she

glanced that direction. AJ stood in the light like some kind of avenging angel. Relief swept through her followed quickly by concern. Kurt was not a man to mess with.

AJ reached out and snatched Bobby up from where he was scooting away from Kurt, his eyes still wide with fear.

"Outside. Run. Hide." AJ wasn't taking any chances with the boy. He pulled him to his feet.

"But Momma—"

"I've got her. Go."

Bobby raced out the door.

AJ looked over to where Courtney huddled on the floor, blood trailing from the corner of her mouth. He balled his hands into fists, and a rage swept through him, stronger than any emotion he'd ever felt.

"You must be the guy she's shacking up with now." Kurt's words held a menacing, taunting tone.

"You must be Kurt, the guy who hits women and little boys."

"Only when she deserves it." Kurt sounded like he believed his words, which only enraged AJ more.

He needed to get Kurt looking at him so

Courtney could get away. He carefully sidestepped away from the door, leaving it open for Courtney to flee through.

"You don't look that tough." He took another step into the house. Kurt circled after him.

"Only a coward would hit someone weaker than they are," he taunted Kurt and stepped back again. The doorway was now open. Kurt swung at him and caught him on the cheek. AJ shook his head, trying to clear his vision, then suddenly reached out and grabbed Kurt, pulling him toward him. "Run, Courtney."

He saw her scramble up off the floor and race out the door.

"That was a stupid thing to do." Kurt yanked away, took two steps toward the corner, and grabbed Bobby's baseball bat leaning against the wall. "Really stupid thing to do." He twirled the bat in a lazy loop then tightened his grasp on it, stepping closer toward AJ. He raised the weapon, but it stopped mid-arc as he swung it behind him.

"I'll take that." Eddie stood in the doorway, Bobby's bat firmly in his hand.

Kurt whirled around. "You again," he growled. He lunged at Eddie and caught him with an uppercut.

Eddie shook his head and rubbed his jaw. "Yes,

me again. I'm not sure you quite understand the definition of a restraining order." Eddie's words were calm as if talking to a child. "It goes like this. You broke it. Your bail is going to be revoked. And I'm adding in assault charges along with kidnapping and anything else I can think of."

"Right, old man. Like you're going to stop me."

"If he doesn't. I will." AJ circled over to stand by Eddie's side.

"Gentlemen. I'll take over." The sheriff stepped up behind them. They moved aside and let him through. "I thought we'd seen the last of you, son."

Kurt looked around the room, searching for an escape.

"Pretty sure the odds of you getting out of here without handcuffs are nonexistent." The sheriff held out a pair of cuffs.

Kurt lunged toward the door, and AJ threw himself at the man, taking him down in a thud of limbs and bodies. Eddie caught one of Kurt's arms, and the sheriff clicked the cuff on his other wrist. They dragged him to his feet, and the sheriff fastened the second cuff.

"I'm getting pretty tired of hauling you off. Let's make sure you just stay in jail from now on, what do you say?"

The sheriff led Kurt out the door. Kurt let out a stream of curse words in his wake.

Eddie turned to AJ. "You okay?"

"I'm fine." He rubbed his cheekbone, fairly certain he'd be sporting a black eye.

Eddie put his arm around AJ's shoulder. "Thank you for getting here so quickly. For helping my family. Come on. Let's find Courtney and Bobby and make sure they're okay." Eddie paused. "And I'm going to make it my mission in life to make sure that man never sees a day out of his jail cell ever again."

AJ thought that was probably the best life mission statement he'd ever heard.

Courtney stood in the middle of the courtyard outside the bungalow with Bobby held tightly in her arms. She savored the feel of him, the scent of him, the way his hands clutched around her neck. She thanked God, the universe, her lucky stars, and anyone else she could think of that this sweet boy was back in her arms.

And she especially thanked AJ.

She looked across the parking lot, watching the sheriff stuff Kurt into the back of his deputy's car. Kurt sent one more menacing glare in her direction.

Tally put her arm around Courtney's shoulder. "Don't you worry about him. We'll make sure he can never come after you again."

"Mr. Hamilton." Bobby wriggled out of her arms and raced across to where AJ and Eddie walked across the courtyard toward them. He threw his arms around AJ.

AJ scooped the boy up and hugged him. "Hey, kiddo. Glad to see you're okay." He frowned. "Are you okay?"

"I'm fine. I'm a tough guy. Kurt doesn't scare me. And Grams said he's gone for good this time."

"He will be. I'll make sure of that." Eddie's words couldn't have sounded more certain.

AJ walked over to her and let Bobby slide to the ground. She couldn't help herself. She knelt down and pulled Bobby into her arms again.

"Courtney, I'm so sorry." AJ's face twisted with guilt.

She shook her head. "No, this wasn't your fault."

"Of course it was. I shouldn't have let Bobby out of my sight. Any grown person knows that much."

Before she could stop AJ's apology, Bobby wrestled free from her grasp and turned to look at her. "Momma, you're gonna be mad at me."

"Oh, honey. I'm not mad at you." She hugged him then trailed her hand along his cheek.

"But… I saw Kurt the other day. On the beach when I was playing with AJ. I saw him, but then I thought I was just *imagining* it. I should have told you, then he wouldn't have gotten me."

"Oh, Bobby. It's not your fault. None of this."

"It was Kurt you thought you saw?" AJ's voice sounded incredulous, and he looked even more guilty if that were even possible. "I had no idea. I thought… it was just part of our game. I should have listened to you better. I messed that one up, too."

"None of this is your fault *or* Bobby's fault. And I'm just grateful you showed up when you did."

"It should never have happened."

"Stop it." Courtney looked up at him. "This is Kurt's doing. Not yours."

Bobby looked up at AJ then, his eyes no longer filled with fear, the tears dried on his face. Her heart finally released its death grip on her breath. Bobby was going to be okay. He'd probably have nightmares again, but with Tally's and Eddie's help, they'd make sure that once again he'd feel safe.

"You saved me again, Mr. Hamilton. You're like a real hero." Bobby grinned up at AJ, his face covered in an adoring smile.

Somehow, AJ didn't feel like anyone's savior. He felt

like a screwup. Kurt should never have been able to get to Bobby, especially when Courtney had entrusted her son to him. And look how that had turned out.

He looked down at the bright red streak across Courtney's face and the swollen lip. Her shirt was torn at the neck. His heart shattered into tiny pieces. He shouldn't have let this happen. "It wouldn't have happened if I hadn't been so—"

"Tell you what. How about we take Bobby to Magic Cafe. I think we could make him up a vanilla shake. How about that?" Tally looked pointedly at him and Courtney. "Courtney, why don't you and AJ go back inside? See if…" She paused and looked down at Bobby. "You might want to clean up. And you two should talk."

"That's a good idea." Courtney stood up shakily.

He wanted to rush over and help her, hold her steady. But he held back, unsure of himself.

"Bobby, you go with Eddie and Tally, and I'll meet you there soon." Courtney kissed Bobby on the top of his head.

"You going to have ice cream too when you come over?"

"You bet. Save me some."

"You should bring Mr. Hamilton, too. You get hungry when you save people, you know."

Courtney gave the boy a tired smile. AJ watched her stand silently as Tally and Eddie took Bobby away. She didn't move until they were out of sight then turned to him. "Come on in."

He did as she asked. The least he could do was help straighten up the mess in her apartment before Bobby got back.

They walked inside, and he saw a broken vase on the floor. A framed photo rested amid a sea of broken glass. A chair was overturned, and Bobby's bat sat on the floor, no longer a menacing weapon, just a small boy's sporting equipment. "I'll clean this up."

"I'll be out to help in a moment. I'm just going to go put on a clean shirt and wash my face." She turned and slowly walked down the hallway to her bedroom.

He straightened the room as best he could, picking up the broken shards of the vase, the pieces of glass, and righting the bat in the corner with Bobby's glove. He paused in his chores and froze in place. The sound of muffled sobs drifted out from Courtney's bedroom.

The tiny pieces of his shattered heart grated inside of him, shredding him raw. He set aside the dustpan and walked down the hallway. "Court?" He knocked on the door. "Can I come in?"

"I—okay."

He pushed the door open. She sat on the floor at the end of the bed, her eyes rimmed in red, tears flowing down her cheeks. He swallowed, trying to catch his breath, trying to survive the surge of pain stabbing through him.

"Ah, Court. I'm so, so sorry." He slipped onto the floor beside her and gently put his arm around her.

"I… I just can't pull myself together." A small sob escaped her swollen lips.

"I don't think you have to. You've been through a lot today. Bobby was missing. And there was Kurt and…" He reached out and, ever so gently, as light as a feather, touched her reddened cheek. "I wish I could have stopped this from happening."

The guilt crushed him, sucking all the oxygen from his lungs. If only he'd kept Bobby with him, held his hand. Or even if he'd asked Bobby more questions when the boy had seen Kurt on the beach. Not just pushed it off as his boyish imagination. AJ just kept making mistakes, and Courtney had paid dearly for them.

She leaned against him, and slowly her sobs subsided. She wiped a hand across her face, streaking the tears, and smiled weakly at him. "There, see. I'm all better."

"You don't have to be better for me." He tried to soothe her with his words.

"I am going to get up now and wash my face and change my shirt. I don't want Bobby to see me like this."

He stood and reached a hand down for her. She slipped her hand in his, which only reminded him that he should have been holding Bobby's hand today.

Every. Single. Minute.

He turned away and left the room, closing the door quietly behind him, knowing what he had to do.

Courtney gave one last look in the bathroom mirror. Her cheek was a bright rosy red, her lips swollen, and a small split was evident on her upper lip. There wasn't much makeup could do to hide it, and the thought of touching her face to put makeup on was more than she could bear. A clean-washed face was it for now.

She shrugged off the torn shirt and held it in her hands, staring at it. In a fit of fury, she balled it up and tossed it in the trash. Bruises showed on her bare skin where Kurt had grabbed her. She shuddered as she rubbed her hands softly up and down her arms.

Hopefully, now he truly would be out of their lives. With one last look at the marks Kurt had left on her body, she hurried out to the bedroom and grabbed a clean shirt, carefully pulling it on, her muscles and bruises screaming in protest.

She was going to be okay, though. She was. So was Bobby. Kurt was not going to ruin the life they had here. He wasn't. She'd do everything in her power to make sure he never, ever got a chance to get near Bobby again.

Feeling empowered with her new resolution, she headed back out to see what damage was done to the apartment and get it straightened up before Bobby got home.

AJ stood by the window, looking out. The room was all picked up, everything back in place. No sign of anything broken. No sign Kurt had ever been here.

"AJ, you didn't have to do all that, but thank you." She crossed the room and stood by him. When he didn't answer, she softly rested her hand on his arm. "I'm so grateful you showed up when you did."

He turned to her, his face a picture of torture. "But I didn't get here soon enough, did I? And I was the one who left Bobby alone so Kurt could get to him. *And* I didn't listen to him about seeing Kurt on the beach. So many mistakes."

"It's not your fault." She didn't know how to reassure him and how many times she'd have to repeat herself.

"But it's a consequence of my actions, my mistakes." He let out a long breath as if he was letting out all the air in his entire body in one pain-filled whoosh. "My father is right about me. I'm just one mistake after the next."

"AJ, don't say that."

"But it's true."

"Come on, let's go get that ice cream at Magic Cafe. We just need time to relax and put this behind us." She pulled on his arm.

He looked straight into her eyes with a stare that seemed to pierce her very soul. "I will never, *ever* get over this. Not what happened to you. Not what Bobby went through. I think it's best…" He turned away, breaking their connection and leaving her instantly adrift. "I think it's best I just leave you two alone. I… I can't do this. My irresponsibility and mistakes… I can't make mistakes that hurt others."

"But—"

He put a finger to her lips and shook his head. "It's for the best. Tell Bobby goodbye for me."

He turned and walked out of the bungalow, closing the door firmly behind him, the sound echoing across the room. She stood by the window, alone, in aching loneliness.

CHAPTER 21

Courtney looked over at Bobby playing at a table in the corner of Magic Cafe. Eddie had brought a board game, and the two of them laughed as they played and drank large glasses of lemonade. Courtney hadn't been able to bear to let Bobby go to his sitter's, and Eddie had watched him the last few days, often hanging out at the restaurant together.

Courtney wandered back to Tally's office to see if she needed any help. Tally looked up from the computer and smiled. There was so much love in Tally's eyes that she grabbed the doorframe in support. That instant love and acceptance, it still caught her off guard. This whole having a family was so new and special and almost magical at times.

"Come, sit. Take a short break." Tally patted the chair next to her desk.

"I came to see if I could help with anything. My waitress shift is over, but I could help out in here with business things. Eddie and Bobby are immersed in a game of Chutes and Ladders. I think they're both cheating." She smiled as she sank onto the offered chair.

"Probably." Tally shoved aside a stack of papers she'd been working on. "So, are you doing okay?"

"I am. At least, I think so."

"The offer still stands to move in with Eddie and me."

She had to admit the offer sounded better and better. Maybe if they'd moved in with her grandparents, all this wouldn't have happened. Maybe her fierce need for independence had contributed to all the trouble with Kurt.

"I recognize that look. You're feeling guilty. Stop it." Tally pushed her chair back from the desk.

"I... I just want to make it on my own. But I know Bobby would love living with you. But I do like our bungalow, and Bobby has friends living only a few doors down." She could probably overthink her decision for hours...

"Well, you decide what you think is best. We fully support any choice you make, you know that."

"Thanks."

Tally sat up straight. "So, tell me. I haven't seen any sign of AJ in a few days. How's he doing?"

"He… I haven't seen him."

A frown crossed her face. "Is he out of town?"

"No… he thought it was better if we don't see each other. I… I think he thinks we're—Bobby and me—too much responsibility. He feels guilty about Kurt taking Bobby and me getting hit." She reached up and touched her cheek, knowing an ugly yellow bruise covered her cheekbone, even though she tried to hide it with makeup.

"I'm sorry he feels so responsible."

"I just… well, I shouldn't have let Bobby get so close to him. Bobby keeps asking where AJ is. And… I don't know how to explain it to him. He's hurt and confused."

"It's a tough thing for a little boy to understand. All the twists and turns of adult relationships."

"Well, I won't make the same mistake again. I really have no desire to date, but if I ever do, I won't let Bobby get involved with whoever I date. I'm not going to let him get hurt again. And AJ didn't even say goodbye to him."

Her heart grabbed in her chest, and exhausted anger pulsed through her, along with guilt for letting Bobby befriend AJ. Now Bobby looked at her with sad eyes when he asked each day if AJ was going to watch him again and play starfish invaders. She learned a powerful lesson at Bobby's expense.

Just how many mistakes could she make with Bobby? She'd made so very, very many. And all she'd ever wanted was to provide him with a better childhood than the one she'd had.

Tally looked at her granddaughter. She was lost in her own thoughts. Tally was pretty sure Courtney was beating herself up about AJ and Bobby. She stood and reached out a hand. "Come on. Let's go out and have some lemonade with Eddie and Bobby. See how their game is going. I bet you're tired and would like to head back to your bungalow."

They went out to the deck and over to where Eddie and Bobby were sitting.

"Hi, Momma. Guess what? I won the last two games."

"You did?"

"Yep."

She and Courtney sat down at the table, and she poured them lemonade and watched while

Eddie and Bobby continued their game. Courtney sat still lost in thought.

Tally looked up to see Delbert Hamilton and Camille standing beside the table. Delbert smiled a wide, good-to-see-you smile. Camille—not so much. Her smile was artificial with a hint of annoyance.

"Good to see all of you." Delbert turned to Bobby. "How've you been, Bobby?"

"I'm fine, Mr. Hamilton. Did you know you have the same name as Momma's Mr. Hamilton?"

Delbert smiled. "I do. He's my cousin."

Bobby frowned. "I don't think I have any of those, do I, Momma?"

"No, afraid not."

"Well, good, then there won't be so many people with the same name as me." He turned back to the game.

"Say, how about you all come to Camille's party this weekend? It's Saturday. I know it's short notice, but we'd love for you to come, wouldn't we, darlin'?"

Tally was pretty sure the expression on Camille's face said she didn't agree with him.

"Oh, I don't know. The cafe is so busy on the weekend." Tally shook her head.

"Oh, but we'd love for you to come." Delbert glanced at Camille.

"Well, if they're busy…" Camille didn't even try to hide her relief at the excuse.

And that annoyed Tally. "Well, I bet we could probably find someone to run the cafe that night. What do you say, Courtney? Wouldn't it be fun to go out?"

"Oh, I don't want to leave Bobby."

"How about I watch Bobby?" Eddie chimed in. "Boys' night. You and Tally go and have a girls' night out."

"Perfect. That's what we'll do." Tally patted her hand on the table in decision.

Camille's eyes flashed in annoyance, and she plastered her fake smile on her perfectly made-up face. "Well, won't that be nice?" she said without a trace of sincerity.

"Well, come on, darlin'. We should go and leave this fine family to their game. We'll see you Saturday night, then, right?"

"Right. We'll be there," Tally assured him.

As soon as they left, Courtney leaned over and whispered to her, low enough so Bobby wouldn't hear. "Why did you say yes? I don't want to go. AJ is probably going to be there."

"Oh, you think so? Perhaps. Oh well, it will be a big party. If he's there, you can just ignore him."

Courtney didn't look convinced.

But maybe if they went, Courtney would get a chance to talk to AJ. Maybe he'd just been scared. Tally didn't blame him. So much had happened that day.

And Courtney didn't fool her one bit. She liked AJ. Liked him a lot.

And Tally liked AJ, too. Her instincts told her he was a good man. She thought he was a good match for Courtney and the first man she'd ever shown an interest in.

This party would be the perfect opportunity for them to have another chance to talk. Maybe they could work things out. Tally was a firm believer in second chances. She glanced over at Eddie, and he looked up and smiled at her. A now-familiar contentment flowed through her, and she smiled back at him.

CHAPTER 22

AJ walked downstairs, dressed in the business casual his grandmother would expect him to wear to Camille's party. He'd spent the last few days sulking in his room and missing Courtney and Bobby, not that there was anything he could do about it. He'd made his decision. It was the best thing for everyone. Especially Courtney and Bobby.

"Ashton, there you are."

"There I am." He walked over and kissed her cheek.

"We have a bit of time, and there's something I'd like to talk to you about."

"What's that?" He eyed her suspiciously.

"It's about you and your father." She patted the couch beside her.

He sat down, dreading the conversation that was sure to come.

"I know you two don't see eye to eye. He's a hard man to please. He expects a lot from everyone, but even more from himself. He *needs* that control in his life now." She paused and looked at him. "But he used to be different, you know. Before your mother died. He tried so hard to save her, but it was out of his control. Now he wants to control… everything."

AJ frowned. He'd never really looked at it from his father's angle, but honestly, he'd never been able to please the man. Ever. He wasn't sure what his grandmother wanted him to say.

"He does love you."

AJ didn't know about that. He was pretty sure his father didn't love anyone.

"He's just afraid to care that much about anyone ever again and get so heartbroken. I've tried to talk to him, but… well, I haven't gotten through. I know you've had a hard time. I know you acted out, causing trouble and running with a fast crowd. But I don't for a minute believe that's the real you." She rested a hand on his. "I would really like it if you and your father could work things out. You could even work for him again."

"I don't think that will ever happen."

"Maybe." She sighed. "But I can hope."

"Why are you bringing this all up now?"

Granice looked directly at him. "Because your father called, and he's going to be at the party tonight." She then stood and picked her purse up from the table. "Well, I don't want to be late."

He sat there in stunned silence, wondering if he could call a cab for his grandmother and send her to the party without him.

"Ashton?"

He slowly pushed off the couch, a mountain of dread crushing down on him.

Courtney and Tally walked up to Camille's enormous beach house. Tiki lights lined the long walk up to the house. Lights were strung along the railing of the immense front deck.

"Look, they actually have valet parking." Courtney pointed to a threesome of young men by the entrance to the driveway.

"Well, there isn't much parking space here. They must have arranged to park the cars off-site. Can't say that I've been to a private party with valet parking before, though." Tally shrugged, and they knocked on the front door.

"Welcome." A man in a suit—which was strange for a beach house party in Florida— motioned them in. "The Montgomerys are on the back deck by the pool. Someone will come by and get your drink order."

"Fancy," Courtney whispered to Tally then looked down at her own simple cotton dress. She smoothed the skirt with a nervous stroke, wondering if she was woefully underdressed.

"Let's go outside." Tally linked her arm in Courtney's, and they headed out to the pool area.

As they stepped out on the wide deck surrounding the pool area, she looked around quickly to see if AJ was there. She couldn't spot him in the crowd, but then the place was packed full of people. Some of the crowd spilled down onto the beach under a large tented area.

Delbert saw them and hurried over. "Welcome. We're really glad you came." He turned and waved Camille over. She didn't look like she wanted to come but pasted on her now-familiar artificial smile.

"Darlin', look, Tally and Courtney are here. Isn't that nice? I do so love your restaurant, Tally."

"Why, thank you. We love having you there." Tally smiled at the compliment.

"Yes, we are *so* glad you came." Camille flashed

perfect white teeth surrounded by a perfect fake smile. "I doubt if you know anyone here, but, well, why don't you grab some drinks?"

"We'll do that." Tally smiled her naturally warm smile, not letting Camille's obvious snub get to her.

Courtney wasn't quite having as much luck. She'd like to get a drink and toss it in the woman's face. She didn't like people acting superior to Tally.

Delbert and Camille walked away to greet other guests, and she and Tally got glasses of white wine from a passing waiter. Courtney took a sip of her drink. "Want to go down on the beach? Maybe it's not so crowded down there."

"Good idea." They headed down the long walkway.

Courtney slipped off her sandals and dropped them at the end of the walkway. She wasn't sure if going barefoot was acceptable at a party like this, but she just didn't care. She hated wearing shoes on the sand. Tally followed her lead and dropped her shoes next to Courtney's.

They wandered under the large white tent. Bar-height tables were scattered around under it with people standing with drinks and appetizers and chatting.

Camille had been right about one thing. Courtney didn't see even one person she knew.

Which was fine with her, because she really, really didn't want to run into AJ. For all she knew, maybe he'd left town. Which was fine with her, too. Or at least she was trying to convince herself of that.

"Courtney, Tally."

She whirled around and came face to face with AJ. Her heart immediately began galloping at such a pace she could barely catch her breath. He stood there in casual khaki slacks and a light blue button-down shirt with the sleeves rolled up. She swallowed, unable to deny the pull he had, the undeniable attraction she felt.

No, she wasn't attracted to him. She wasn't. He'd made their relationship perfectly clear...

They didn't have one.

So she felt... *nothing*... toward him.

"AJ, so nice to see you. I've missed you at Magic Cafe. Hope you haven't tired of my grouper and hushpuppies." Tally smiled at him as if it was perfectly fine for him to be standing here talking to them.

"Not a bit. I've just..." He looked at Courtney. "I've been busy."

"Well, come by soon," Tally insisted.

AJ didn't answer her but sent her a look that was half smile, half wistful, and tinged with sadness.

"Ashton, there you are. Mother said you'd be out here."

They all turned toward the man who'd come up behind them. He was dressed in dress slacks with an impeccable crease ironed into them. His freshly shaven face had a hard edge to it. His dark hair was streaked with gray.

"Father." AJ said the word with less enthusiasm than even Camille had displayed when welcoming them to the party.

AJ stepped closer to Courtney and draped his arm around her shoulder. She almost dropped her drink. "Father, this is my girlfriend, Courtney, and her grandmother, Tally. This is my father, Jacob Hamilton."

His father's eyes narrowed, then he nodded at them. "Nice to meet you." A perfect, business-toned reply.

Courtney was getting a bit tired of all the insincere tones at the party. She turned and looked right into AJ's eyes, wondering what in the world was going on with him. She couldn't miss his pleading look, but she wasn't ready to play his games. Not after he'd left her standing alone in her bungalow. Not after he hadn't even said goodbye to Bobby.

"I'm not exactly his girlfriend…"

227

"Yes." His father just said the one word, and she was unclear what a single word meant in reply to her correction to AJ's claim.

"I need to talk to my son," AJ's father commanded all of them.

"We'll wait until later. I don't think this party is the right time." AJ stood his ground against the formidable man. Courtney couldn't help being a bit impressed.

"Now." The man didn't back down either.

"Later." AJ's tone was just as insistent.

"Well, if you want me to talk in front of your *girlfriend*, fine. I saw your photo in the paper. We had an agreement. I'm so disappointed in you."

"Of course you are." AJ dropped his arm from around her shoulder and slipped his hands in his pockets.

"I said that your trust fund was going to be shut off if you got into any more trouble. I sent you to this island, away from... well, away from everything. You still managed to get in trouble with the law and hit the gossip page."

Courtney waited for AJ to explain that he'd been *helping* the woman at the bar, but he stood in stony silence.

When AJ didn't say anything, she turned to his father. "Sir, it wasn't—"

AJ held up a hand. "No."

"But—"

"It doesn't matter, Court." His voice left no doubt. She should drop it.

She looked at AJ in bewilderment. Of course, it mattered. He'd done a good thing. A heroic thing. And he'd helped her get away from Kurt, too. He wasn't someone his father should be disappointed in, he was someone his father should be proud of, even if she was angry with him for just walking out of her life and Bobby's.

Though, she knew exactly how AJ felt. Sometimes no matter what you did, you couldn't please someone. That was exactly like how it had been with her maternal grandmother. She didn't know the dynamics going on here, but if AJ wanted her to drop it, she would.

But she didn't have to like it.

CHAPTER 23

AJ's pulse burned through him at the public dressing-down his father had given him in front of Courtney. Though, it was his own fault. He should have known his father wouldn't take "we'll talk later" for an answer. He could feel Courtney stiffen at his side, but he didn't want her to come to his rescue. Nothing would change his father's opinion of him, and maybe the man was right, anyway. He'd certainly let down Courtney and Bobby.

Just then, as if things weren't complicated and awkward enough, another man and a young woman approached. He looked closely at the woman who looked vaguely familiar.

She walked up and kissed him on the cheek.

"Daddy, this is the man I was telling you about, the man who saved me from that drunk at the club."

He recognized her then. Lynn Miller from the club in Sarasota.

"Jacob?" The man with Lynn turned to his father.

Much to AJ's surprise, the two men embraced and clapped each other on the back. "Ron Miller, I haven't seen you since our days at Harvard Business School."

"Good to see you. So, this young man is your son?"

AJ watched as his father slowly nodded.

"Well, he saved my girl here from a run-in with a lousy drunk at a club in Sarasota a week or so back." The man turned to AJ and put out his hand. "I'm forever grateful for your protection. She ended up with a nasty bruise, but it could have been so much worse. If I can ever, ever do anything for you, you let me know."

AJ's father stared at him in amazement. "You were protecting her?"

"Yes, sir."

"Why didn't you say…" His father's words trailed off, and though AJ had never once seen this look on his father's face, he'd swear the man was *embarrassed*, possibly even sorry.

But that didn't fit in with his reality of the man who was his father. Not at all.

"What do you say, Jacob? Let's go grab a drink and catch up on the last… well, on a lot of years."

"Yes." His father started to walk away with the man but paused and looked back at AJ. "We'll talk later."

Lynn smiled at him. "Well, I'm going to catch up with my friends over there." She waved to a group of women. "But I wanted to say thank you again."

"It was nothing."

"It was to me." She turned and headed over to her friends.

Courtney and Tally still stood next to him, watching the conversations, not saying a word.

"Sorry about the girlfriend remark, Court. I was just trying to avoid that whole ugly scene here at Camille's party."

He thought he saw pity, or at the very least sympathy, in Courtney's eyes. The last thing he wanted to see.

"Well, you two excuse me, I think I'll go track down another drink." Tally started to walk away.

"No, I'll send a waiter over." He waved down a server who headed their direction. "I was leaving anyway." He turned and fled the party, walking rapidly down to the shoreline and along the water's edge, not caring that the waves were splashing water all over his slacks.

He just needed to escape. Escape his father. Escape Courtney's pity.

The moon ducked behind a cloud, plunging him into near darkness. If only it was possible for him to hide behind a cloud forever.

Courtney watched AJ walk away. A heaviness draped over her heart. She knew exactly how he felt about disappointing his father. About someone you cared about thinking the worst of you, and it hurt. It hurt deeply.

"That was quite a scene." Tally stood by her side, also watching AJ walk out onto the beach. "His father was kind of harsh, wasn't he?"

"He was."

"You know, it looks like AJ has had a long time of hearing he's done things wrong. That's a hard litany to get out of your brain."

"I know."

Tally put a hand on her arm. "I know you do. I'm sorry you went through the same thing with your other grandmother. I'd give anything if I could change that."

She nodded.

"I think that AJ's father, and the way the man talks to him… well, it might have factored into his decision to stop seeing you and Bobby."

"What do you mean?"

"Well, if someone has always said that you've screwed up, you start to believe them. When AJ lost Bobby and he couldn't protect you from Kurt, well, those words that have been pounded into him probably took over. He thought he did wrong. Took responsibility for what happened. Thought he could have done something—I don't know—better or different and things wouldn't have happened the way they did."

"I do still hear my other grandmother's voice playing over and over in my mind."

"Well, I certainly hope you don't listen to it. You're a fabulous young woman, a wonderful mother, and you are mightily loved by Eddie and me."

Courtney hugged Tally. "I love you guys, too."

She looked at the woman who had been more a grandmother to her in the last few months than her maternal grandmother who had raised her had been through all her childhood. "Can I ask you something?"

"Of course."

"I… I wondered if… could I call you Grams like Bobby does? And call Eddie, Pops?"

Tally leaned forward and grabbed both of her hands. "Of course you can. We'd love that."

Courtney didn't miss the hint of a tear in the corner of her grandmother's eye. She squeezed Tally's—*Grams'*—hands.

"I've waited my whole life for this and never thought I'd get it after your father died. You and Bobby have brought so much happiness to my life." Her grandmother's face glowed with joy.

"Eddie's probably responsible for a lot of that happiness, too." She smiled.

"That too." Tally looked around the party. "What do you say we blow this place? Let's go back home and have ice cream with Eddie and Bobby, what do you say?"

"I say that's a wonderful idea." They linked arms and walked back through the house and out down the tiki torch-lined walkway.

But Courtney couldn't erase the look she'd seen on AJ's face when his father had berated him in front of them. A look she was sure had been on her own face many times over the years.

AJ needed someone like Tally in his life who gave him love unconditionally. *Everyone* needed someone like Tally in their lives.

CHAPTER 24

The next morning, AJ briefly considered hiding out in his room and avoiding his father and grandmother, but he decided he was finished with that.

AJ tromped down the stairs and into the great room. His father stood at the window, sipping a cup of coffee. He turned when he heard AJ enter the room. "Morning, son. I've been waiting to talk to you."

His grandmother got up from her seat on the couch. "I'm going to leave you two alone. I think you have a lot to talk about."

AJ walked over to the coffeepot and poured himself a cup. He steeled himself for whatever scolding his father would dish out. One thing he'd decided, though. He was leaving Belle Island today.

No more grounding. He didn't give a whit about the trust fund. Let the man take the whole thing from him. He'd already set up three interviews for jobs. He'd be fine. He'd make it on his own without anyone's threats or demands.

"AJ—I was talking to Delbert last night and he said you prefer to be called AJ—might take me a bit to get used to it. Anyway, son, I need to say some things to you."

"Save it, Father. I'm just not interested anymore. Take the trust. Do what you want."

"No, *please*. Listen to me."

He couldn't miss the urgency in his father's voice, so he leaned against the counter with one hip and waited for him to continue.

"Your grandmother said you'd been seeing that Courtney woman, but then you stopped. What happened?"

"Things went wrong." He wasn't going to get into the details with the man.

"But you like her, don't you? I have my faults— many of them—but I'm pretty good at reading people. You care about her, don't you?"

"It doesn't matter. It wouldn't work out."

"Ashton—AJ, please listen to me, and if you want to leave after this, I won't stand in your way."

His father came and leaned against the counter across from him.

AJ wanted to just turn and walk away, ignore that his father wanted to talk, show his father that he didn't dance to his tune anymore. But then it all came down to one thing. The man still was his father.

His father set his coffee cup on the counter. "Don't wall off like I did. I've always been hard on you. Judgmental. I'm sorry. I think I did it to push you away. Then…" His father's eyes clouded with pain. "Then, you'd have no chance to leave me like… your mother did. It makes no rational sense. But nothing about your mother dying and a world without her made any sense to me. I threw myself into my work and wanted perfection from everyone. I needed control over everything."

AJ set his own coffee down and stared at this man standing before him, a stranger, certainly not his father. His father would never be this… *honest* with him.

"If your mother could see what a mess I've made with my relationship with you… she'd never forgive me. Will you give me another chance? Please? I am proud of you. I am. I've been such a fool. I just… I'm so sorry. I know I can't ever make up for what I've put you through, but I'm deeply, deeply sorry for all the mistakes I've made."

He wanted to look around to see if there was a hidden camera, if this was some kind of trick, if his real father would reappear.

"I… I don't know what to say." He gripped the counter behind him with both hands, holding on for balance, sure the world was spinning backward now.

"You don't have to say anything. You don't have to forgive me… how I've treated you isn't really forgivable. I had a long talk with Ron last night. He's always been a straight shooter. He made me see… well, what a fool I've been."

AJ didn't think he trusted this new version of Jacob Hamilton.

"And I know I fired you from the company. Without listening to you, of course. I've come to realize you quit trying to defend yourself from my often wrong snap decisions I make of your actions. I know why you made the decision you did. The one that made me fire you. You were covering for Sam Diamond, weren't you? He screwed up the numbers on the acquisition, and you took the blame so I wouldn't fire him."

"How did you find out?"

"Sam came to me and told me what

happened. His wife was ill, and he needed the health insurance. They would have lost it if he got fired."

AJ nodded.

"And I'm embarrassed to think I was the kind of boss who would fire a person for one mistake, but I'm sure I would have."

"So, did you fire him after he told you the truth?" AJ narrowed his eyes.

"No, I figured the stress in his life caused his lapse in his normal attention to detail. He's still with me. Promoted him, actually. And his wife, Carlene, is much better now."

"You know his wife's name?" AJ was sure his mouth was hanging open in surprise. His father rarely learned the names of his employees, much less their wives.

"I know." His father grinned.

Grinned.

He was absolutely positive he'd never seen his father grin. Ever.

"Now, I hope you'll accept my apology and you'll give me a second chance. And while we're talking. Do not shut yourself off from people. Don't wall yourself off from a good thing because I was such a colossal screwup raising you. I think you need to give that Courtney woman another chance.

243

Second chances, I've come to believe in them." There was that *grin* again.

He took a deep breath, made a leap of faith, and held out his hand. "Yes, okay. Let's start over."

His father crossed the distance, grabbed his hand, then wrapped him in a hug. "I'm so sorry, son."

"It's okay. We'll be okay." And for the first time since the day his mother died, he truly believed he and his father would be okay. They'd find a way to build back a relationship. AJ wanted nothing more than that in his life.

No, wait. That was a lie.

CHAPTER 25

AJ hurried over to Courtney's bungalow, hoping she'd talk to him. Hoping… hoping she'd believe second chances were just as important as his father did.

She opened the door to his knock and glanced back into the room. "Bobby, I'm going to step outside. You can play your video game for fifteen minutes before we head to Grams' and Pops'."

He heard Bobby's voice through the open doorway. "Yes!"

He smiled. He could picture Bobby's excited pumping of his arm as he raced to the gaming machine to turn it on.

Courtney stepped outside. "I don't want Bobby to see you. It's been hard on him. I should never have—"

"No, *I* should never have. I shouldn't have just run off like that. Dropped both of you from my life. I just felt so guilty I hadn't protected you. That my mistakes had caused you pain." He drew in a deep breath. "But, if you give me a second chance, I won't run off again. I swear. I've missed you. Both you and Bobby. I was scared to mess up again. Afraid my mistakes would harm you again. I don't know anything about... well, taking care of people. I've only ever taken care of myself."

"It wasn't your mistake. I told you this was all Kurt's fault, not yours."

His heart pounded in his chest, soaring with hope. "So, you'll give me a second chance?"

She looked at him for what seemed like an eternity. He couldn't read her eyes, couldn't read her expression.

And then he could.

"I'm sorry. I just can't. Bobby was crushed when you just walked out of our lives. I can't take that chance with him again. Can't let him get hurt. I don't even want him to see you or know you've been here. Please, just go. It's what's best for Bobby, and what's best for him will always be my first choice. Please, just leave us alone." She turned and slipped inside.

The pain of her refusal crushed him, made it

impossible to breathe, to think. He'd come to care about her and Bobby so deeply in the last few weeks. He'd never believed it when people said they knew, truly knew, within days of meeting someone, that they were the right person.

But now he believed it.

But he'd messed it up. Lost his chance.

He stumbled across the courtyard, down the road to the beach, and out to the water's edge, walking aimlessly along the beach, not paying any attention to where he was going. Knowing this was his fault, not Courtney's. He couldn't blame her for protecting Bobby. Her putting Bobby first was just one of the things he loved about her.

Loved.

He stopped, and a wave splashed up on him, but he paid no attention to it.

He loved her.

He. Loved. Courtney.

Which only made the pain that much more unbearable. Then he knew what he needed to do. He raced down the beach to the lighthouse.

When he got there, he bent over, trying to catch his breath. As his breath steadied, he looked up at it. Regal. Standing as a protector of the island.

Without stopping to think about how practical it was, he reached down and picked up a good-sized shell. He opened his palm and stared down at it. The shell was chipped into the shape of a perfect heart.

He closed his eyes, made a wish, and tossed the shell out into the sea. He looked at the lighthouse one more time, hoping against all hope the legend was true.

Courtney and Tally trailed behind Eddie and Bobby as they all walked along the beach that afternoon. Simple moments like this, they were the moments Courtney lived for. It was enough. She didn't need AJ or any man.

But her heart squeezed in her chest every time she realized she'd told him to go. She'd never see him again. She looked up at the lighthouse looming over them. The one that promised to answer your deepest desires. She paused as Tally continued on.

Taking a deep breath, she reached down to pick up a shell and clasp it tightly in her hand. Only what did she even want? What would she wish for? She had so much in her life already.

But… she missed AJ. His dazzling smile, his laugh, his kiss… and the way he was with Bobby.

But she'd made the right decision. She *had*.

"Convince me I've made the right choice." She tossed the shell into the sea.

She looked up when she heard Bobby give out one of his whoops.

"Mr. Hamilton." Bobby went racing down the beach and leapt into AJ's arms. "There you are. I missed you."

She glared at the lighthouse. This was *not* the way to convince her. She hurried to catch up with Bobby, trying to figure out how to repair the damage of Bobby seeing AJ again. They were in for long days of him asking where Mr. Hamilton was after AJ left the island.

"Momma, look who I found. He didn't leave. He's right here."

AJ let Bobby slide to the ground. "I… didn't know you'd be here. I wanted one last walk to the lighthouse."

"Did you make a wish? They come true here, you know." Bobby danced around all of them.

"Do they?"

"Of course." Bobby nodded wisely. "Whatcha wish for?"

AJ looked directly at Courtney. "I wished for… something I can't have. Something—*someone* —I… love."

Her eyes flew open wide.

249

"I wished I hadn't made a foolish mistake. I wished for a second chance."

"That's a *lot* of wishes."

AJ nodded. "Well, they are really all kind of the same wish."

Tally stood with a hint of a smile on her face. "Come on, Bobby. Let's go up past the lighthouse. We'll come back and get your mom."

Bobby stared at her and cocked his head to one side. "She does look funny. I guess she's tired. Sometimes she gets like that." He skipped off down the beach.

"We'll be back in a bit." Tally squeezed her shoulder, leaned close, and whispered, "The best thing we can ever do is listen to our heart. It never steers us wrong."

Tally and Eddie hurried off down the beach after Bobby.

She turned to look at AJ.

He gave her one of his dazzling smiles. "I hear there's a legend that if you make a wish at Lighthouse Point, and throw a shell into the ocean, your wish will come true."

"I just made a wish that the lighthouse would tell me I made the right decision sending you away."

He reached out and took one of her hands.

"Maybe it's telling you that you made the *wrong* decision. Maybe it's trying to… make things right."

"I'm scared to make the wrong decision. Scared to make a mistake that will hurt Bobby."

"I know how you feel. I'm scared too." He reached out and touched her face. "But we can face our fears together."

"When you said you wished for someone you… love…"

"I was talking about you." He put his hands on her shoulders and looked directly into her eyes, into the very center of her being. "I love you." His eyes told her everything she needed to know. He was speaking the truth. She could see the love in the depths of his eyes.

And she knew, without a doubt, that she loved this man standing before her, baring his soul, risking rejection, taking a chance.

"I love you too." She smiled up at him, giving him her heart in return, sure in her decision.

He leaned down and kissed her. The waves rushed up around them, encircling their legs, entwining them together as one. He pulled her close to him and held her against his chest. His voice was a gentle whisper in her ear. "Those were the words I wanted to hear. So, you'll give me a second chance?"

"I'll give *us* a second chance. We've both made mistakes."

"We'll do better this time." He released his hold on her, tilted her face up, and kissed her.

"Momma." Bobby came running up to them. "Mr. Hamilton kissed you."

She smiled down at her son. "Yes, he did."

"Huh." He screwed up his face and looked from one of them to the other. "Well, that's cool. Does that mean he's staying and he'll play starfish invaders with me?"

"That's what it means, and so much more." AJ reached out and swooped Bobby up in his arms. The three of them laughed and grinned, spinning in circles, while the waves danced at their feet. They stopped their crazy swirling as Tally and Eddie came up to them with grand smiles spread across their faces.

Eddie leaned over and kissed Tally. "Life just keeps getting better and better, doesn't it?"

CHAPTER 26

Tally stood beside Courtney, marveling at her granddaughter in the simple but oh-so-right-for-her wedding dress. "You look lovely, dear."

"You think so?" Courtney clasped the gold pocket watch hanging from a chain around her neck, setting off the neckline perfectly.

"I think so."

"Bobby is so excited to be AJ's best man." Courtney's eyes shone brightly, and Tally was so happy at this very moment, she felt her very heart might burst.

She never thought she'd have a family, and then she'd found Eddie and Courtney and Bobby. Now Courtney was adding AJ to their family. Tally already thought of him as a son.

She turned at the sound of a knock on the door. Julie and Susan came in.

"Oh, Courtney. You're just beautiful. Let me see the dress, turn around." Susan crossed the room.

"Thank you. It feels a bit unreal." Courtney turned slowly, showing off the vintage wedding dress as asked.

"It was so nice of you to give Courtney the dress you wore to your own wedding, Julie." Tally smiled at her friend.

"Well, it has a rich history of giving people happy lives, so I wanted to share. Besides, that dress really suits Courtney, doesn't it?"

"I love it." Courtney turned and looked in the full-length mirror again. "It's just perfect."

"I put the letter from the original bride back in the hidden pocket again. I figured the note was part of its charm."

Courtney reached into the pocket, slipped out the note, and read it out loud.

I don't know who will end up with this wedding dress of mine. I was married to the love of my life in December 1950. We were married for sixty-two years before he passed away. I'm moving to a nursing home now and must part with my beloved dress. I hope it finds just the right person and I pray that whoever ends up with this dress finds as much happiness as I did.

I wish you a beautiful wedding and years of love.

With much love and blessings for your life together,

Barbara

Tears threatened to fill Courtney's eyes. "This dress means so much to me. Such history. Thank you for sharing it."

"It really, really suits you." Julie crossed over and placed her arm around Courtney's shoulder. "I hope it brings you as much happiness as it did this Barbara so many years ago and it did me."

Courtney took a deep breath. "I better not start crying already."

Susan laughed. "If you start crying, then Tally will."

Courtney laughed, too. "And, Julie, thank you so much for making that gorgeous wedding cake."

"I was happy to."

"This is just… the best day ever." Courtney twirled around in the dress again.

They all laughed.

Tally looked at her two best friends and her

granddaughter and couldn't imagine a life without them. Or Eddie and Bobby.

Susan looked over at her and smiled. "You doing okay there, Tally?"

"I am perfect." She squeezed Susan's hand then turned to Courtney. "Are you ready to do this?"

"I am so ready."

"We'll go tell them to start the music." Julie linked her arm in Susan's, and they headed out the door.

Tally leaned over and kissed Courtney's cheek. "You're going to have a wonderful life. I can feel it. Filled with so much joy."

"Oh, Grams, I feel it, too. AJ makes me so happy. And he's so wonderful with Bobby. I'm so lucky."

Tally thought they'd all had a very lucky year and much happiness had found them. She was grateful every day for the blessing they'd all found.

Her new family. Eddie, Courtney, Bobby, and now AJ.

She opened the door and music spilled into the room. Eddie stood just outside with a broad smile on his face. He held out his arm to Courtney. "You ready?"

Courtney took his arm, her face aglow with

excitement and joy. "I'm ready. I never thought I'd have a grandfather to walk me down the aisle."

"I can't think of walking you toward a finer young man." Eddie leaned down and kissed Courtney's cheek.

Tally slipped past them and walked to her seat. She turned as the music changed and Eddie and Courtney came walking down the aisle. She glanced at AJ and saw he had tears in his eyes as he watched his bride walking toward him.

Eddie turned to AJ when they reached the arbor. "Take care of her."

"I will." AJ took Courtney's hand and squeezed it.

Eddie walked over to stand by Tally, took one look at her, and handed her a handkerchief from his pocket.

She'd thought marrying Eddie was the happiest day of her life… but this day was so special.

Her heart swelled, and tears of joy rolled down her cheeks. She dabbed at them with Eddie's handkerchief, and he looked down at her and smiled a look that told her he was feeling the exact emotions she was. He took her hand in his, his strong fingers wrapping around hers, connecting them.

Bobby handed the wedding bands to the

minister, concentration etched on his tiny face. As soon as he handed them over, he let out a long breath of relief.

She watched as Courtney and AJ said their vows. Their voices strong and true, love evident in each and every word they spoke.

"You are now husband and wife."

"Whoop." Bobby jumped up and down and did a quick fist pump.

AJ kissed Courtney then turned to Bobby and held out his hand. "Come on, son."

Bobby walked down the aisle between AJ and Courtney. Tally didn't even try to hide her tears.

T*wo months later*

"Hurry up, Bobby. We have a surprise for you," Courtney called to her son. She looked up at AJ's face, filled with boyish excitement. She wasn't convinced AJ wasn't more excited about the surprise than Bobby was sure to be.

AJ leaned down and kissed her. "I love you, Mrs. Hamilton."

"I love *you*, Mr. Hamilton."

She couldn't be more sure of her decision to marry this man. They'd moved into a small beach house near Tally and Eddie. AJ had started working at Magic Cafe, helping run it with her while Tally and Eddie began taking frequent trips together, Tally claiming it was a semi-retirement for her. Her grandmother always came back refreshed, eyes sparkling with love for Eddie.

"What's my surprise?" Bobby came skidding into the room.

"It's in the kitchen, go look."

Bobby raced into the kitchen.

AJ laughed as he pulled her along after Bobby.

"Momma, AJ! Did you know there's a puppy in the kitchen?"

They walked into the kitchen, and Bobby had plopped on the floor with the puppy crawling all over him.

"Hm… a puppy. Wonder whose puppy that is?"

"Is it mine? I'm 'sponsible, you know. Very, very 'sponsible."

"Yep, it's yours." AJ knelt down on the floor beside Bobby. The puppy licked his face, and he chuckled the rich tones of his laugh. The one she'd come to love. The one she heard all the time now.

"Do I get to name him? Is it a him?"

"It's a him." Courtney pulled Bobby's excitement around her like a beloved quilt, wrapping their life in love and contentment.

"Oh, and I have another surprise for you and your mother."

"You do?" Bobby looked up from where the puppy was crawling into his lap.

"You do?" She eyed AJ, wondering what he was up to.

"Yep." AJ stood. "I'm taking you and your mother on a trip this winter."

"Where to?"

"We're going skiing in Colorado."

Her eyes opened wide. "Really? Skiing?"

"And I'm going too, this time? You didn't let me go on your honeymoon. Grams said honeymoons are just for adults."

"This one is a *family* vacation."

"Whoop." Bobby stood, picking up the puppy in his arms as he scurried to his feet. "I'm going on a family vacation. My first one ever."

"It won't be our last," AJ promised. "We're going to Sweet River Falls in Colorado. I'll teach you both to ski."

"I bet I'm gonna be good at it."

"I have no doubt." AJ ruffled Bobby's hair.

Bobby sat back down and let the puppy crawl on him.

AJ walked over and stood behind her, his arms

encircling her waist. "Are you happy?" His voice was warm with love.

"I've never been happier." She leaned against him. "You remembered our talk about how much I wanted to try skiing."

"I did. I remember everything about you. I want to spend the rest of my life making you happy."

A sigh escaped her lips. "You do make me happy."

"I'm really glad I went out to Lighthouse Point and made that wish. I'm glad I wished for you to give me a second chance, to love me."

"I'm so glad you did, too." She turned in his arms and leaned up to kiss him, this man she loved so much, this man who'd made the three of them a family. Well, a family of five counting Tally and Eddie, who'd welcomed AJ as a son. Her life had fallen perfectly into place.

"I love you." She reached up to touch his face, and he covered her hand with his own.

"I love you, too. You and Bobby are my whole world."

Love, a family, a perfect life on Belle Island. All her dreams had come true... even the ones she'd never known she'd had.

And the legend of Lighthouse Point lives on for all who believe in it.

Watch for the charming new series, Sweet River, coming soon.

THANK YOU for reading my story. I hope you enjoyed it. Sign up for my newsletter to be updated with information on new releases, promotions, give-aways, and special newsletter-only surprises. The signup is at my website, kaycorrell.com.

Reviews help other readers find new books. I always appreciate when my readers take time to leave an honest review.

I love to hear from my readers. Feel free to contact me at authorcontact@kaycorrell.com

COMFORT CROSSING ~ THE SERIES

The Shop on Main - Book One

The Memory Box - Book Two

The Christmas Cottage - A Holiday Novella (Book 2.5)

The Letter - Book Three

The Christmas Scarf - A Holiday Novella (Book 3.5)

The Magnolia Cafe - Book Four

The Unexpected Wedding - Book Five

The Wedding in the Grove (crossover short story between series - Josephine and Paul from The Letter.)

LIGHTHOUSE POINT ~ THE SERIES

Wish Upon a Shell - Book One

Wedding on the Beach - Book Two

Love at the Lighthouse - Book Three

Cottage near the Point - Book Four

Return to the Island - Book Five

Bungalow by the Bay - Book Six

INDIGO BAY ~ a multi-author series of sweet romance

Sweet Sunrise - Book Three

Sweet Holiday Memories - A short holiday story

Sweet Starlight - Book Nine

ABOUT THE AUTHOR

Kay writes sweet, heartwarming stories that are a cross between women's fiction and contemporary romance. She is known for her charming small towns, quirky townsfolk, and enduring strong friendships between the women in her books.

Kay lives in the Midwest of the U.S. and can often be found out and about with her camera, taking a myriad of photographs which she likes to incorporate into her book covers. When not lost in her writing or photography, she can be found spending time with her ever-supportive husband, knitting, working in her garden, or playing with her puppies—two cavaliers and one naughty but adorable Australian shepherd. Kay and her husband also love to travel. When it comes to vacation time, she is torn between a nice trip to the beach or the mountains—but the mountains only get considered in the summer—she swears she's allergic to snow.

Learn more about Kay and her books at
kaycorrell.com

While you're there, sign up for her newsletter to
hear about new releases, sales, and giveaways.

WHERE TO FIND ME:
kaycorrell.com
authorcontact@kaycorrell.com

Join my Facebook Reader Group. We have lots of
fun and you'll hear about sales and new releases
first!
https://www.facebook.com/groups/KayCorrell/

42946164R00163

Made in the USA
Middletown, DE
18 April 2019